THE DARK MAGE

THE DARK MAGE

HAND OF JUSTICE™ BOOK ONE

JACE MITCHELL

MICHAEL ANDERLE

To my best friend, Tucker.

--Jace

*To Family, Friends and
Those Who Love
to Read.
May We All Enjoy Grace
to Live the Life We Are
Called.*

— Michael

"He's a jackass! I can't believe the Prefect actually let him appear in court," William Teller grumbled as he paced back and forth across the courtyard in the moonlight.

Riley Trident watched him. "You're going to give yourself a heart attack, William. You're not as young as you used to be, and all this quick movement combined with stress might just kill you." Riley grinned. William was about fifteen years older than her, and the only other Right Hand in New Perth.

"On your best day, you're not as good as me on my fuckin' worst," William quipped.

Riley smiled wider, although the big man didn't see it.

They both were clearly in peak shape, even if he *was* older than her. William and Riley were deadly assassins of New Perth's Prefect, whom William served—and the Assistant Prefect, whom Riley served.

As Right Hands, they weren't *just* assassins, though. Nor were they knights, per se. Rather, they were special envoys for New Perth's rulers. Whatever needed to happen, the Right Hands made it so. In the overall hierarchy, William was higher than Riley due to whom he served. Serving the Assistant Prefect was a stupendous achievement, but until Prefect Ire retired or passed away, Riley would be second in the order.

Which was fine with her. She only wanted to serve the court—and Assistant Prefect Mason specifically—in whatever way was needed.

"Why did you call me out here so late to talk about this bullshit?" William asked, still pacing the cobblestone walkway.

"Because, unlike you, I actually listen to people, and I listened to that man today." Riley couldn't stop grinning. This was getting under William's skin, and she loved it.

"You listened to him, huh? Then you must think he's crazy, too? Because otherwise, you're just as crazy."

"That's what I'm not sure about. What if he's *not* crazy?" Riley asked.

William shook his head. Physically, he was the complete opposite of Riley.

To which William always replied, *"Means you got no business bein' a Right Hand. You're too skinny."*

Riley always responded with, *"I'm twice as good as you at half your age."*

For two Right Hands, they were negative images of one another. Where William relied on massive strength and brute force, Riley leaned on speed, agility, and accuracy. Where he looked like a giant, Riley was lithe. Where he was forty, Riley was only twenty-five.

The Prefect's son Mason had chosen Riley, and there was nothing anyone could do about it.

"How could the man *not* be crazy?" William asked, continuing their conversation. "He was in court this morning talkin' about some mage up north. I'm beginning to wonder if *you* were actually listening?"

"I was," Riley answered.

"I'm going to Prefect Ire. We have to get your head tested, because you're clearly losin' your mind, too. Out of two Right Hands, how is only one of them sane?" A small grin appeared at the corner of William's mouth. "Clearly I've always been better with my sword, but now your mind is turnin' to mush right along with your physical skills."

"I'm not saying I believe him, William," Riley countered. "I'm saying maybe we should listen a little harder than we did. I mean, the man barely had finished his plea to Prefect Ire before you threw him through the court's doors."

"You're just mad that you don't have the strength to throw anyone," William retorted, the grin growing wider.

"Keep up that talk and I'll throw *you*, old man." Riley laughed.

The person they were discussing had come to court today to discuss his concerns in front of Prefect Goland Ire. The Prefect ruled New Perth and allowed the citizens to plead before him once a month, feeling that he needed to hear from his people directly. The man William was raving about had had…*abnormal* concerns. They weren't about the rising price of bread or the potholes on a side street.

"Riley," William continued, "for one, I don't like that dirt-covered rats from the street get to say their piece before such a great man. He's given them everythin' they could ask for, and still, they want more. However, that guy today was out of his fuckin' mind. He said a mage up north had *kidnapped* people and was stealing their *magic*. He was using their magic to amplify his *own!* That's ludicrous, Riley. Absolutely ludicrous!"

"Okay, okay, chubby. I hear what you're saying." Riley nodded. "It does seem ludicrous, but he sounded like *he* believed it, didn't he? I mean, if he *is* crazy, I don't think he was lying in that he knew he was telling a falsehood. He *believed* it."

"Your head is soft, skinny. Should we follow every single concern that crosses Prefect Ire's ears just because a crazy person believes it's true? What if someone comes next month sayin' they got ghosts in their blood? Should we deploy doctors to look at 'em?"

Riley sighed, truly wanting to throttle the big man. His mind was made up, and he wasn't going to listen to her.

"I'm just saying, it bothers me how *strongly* he believed it. He was practically screaming at us that we had to listen to him because the mage was coming here next."

William laughed. "We're going to have to see if we can find a replacement Right Hand. You might be good with that sword, skinny, but your head is as soft as fuckin' puddin'.'"

Riley turned swiftly, hearing movement on the other side of the courtyard's door. Nothing got past her senses, even when she was in deep conversation.

The door opened, and one of Mason's servants entered.

"Right Hands," the woman greeted them both, looking down at the ground out of respect.

Riley was the first female Right Hand in the history of New Perth, and she took great honor in that. She was humbled, to be honest. As of this moment, there were only two Right Hands in the city because the Prefect had only one son.

Riley looked at the servant in front of her now. Many people in the court didn't remember those with positions less than their own, but Riley always did. Riley shouldn't have risen so high since she had started even more humbly than this servant.

She knew what it was like to come from nothing, so she simply never overlooked those beneath her.

"Hi, Charlotte." Riley smiled. "Does Mason need me?"

"Yes, Right Hand." Charlotte always used Riley's title, and Riley always told her the same thing.

"Please, Charlotte, call me Riley. We both serve the kingdom. There is no difference between us. They just gave me a sword to carry."

Charlotte nodded and smiled but said nothing, both of them knowing she would call her "Right Hand" the next time they spoke.

"I'll be right there." Riley let Charlotte leave the courtyard, then grinned at William. "What do you want to bet he's thinking the same thing as me?"

"He might be, and I ain't gonna speak ill of the Assistant Prefect, but this is nuts. That man is nuts. And *you* are definitely nuts."

It was ten at night, and Mason hardly ever summoned Riley this late.

"I'll let you know what he says, chubby."

Riley left the courtyard, heading to Mason's quarters.

She was already wearing appropriate attire: her sword and robe. It was a deep purple garment that fell to just above her feet and was much better suited to her style of fighting than William's. She could move easily beneath the cloth, striking out with her sword at a moment's notice. It was like fighting draped in air, and she actually preferred it to the armor that decorum called for sometimes.

Riley reached Mason's door. Charlotte was sitting outside with a book in her hand. She placed the book down and stood up as Riley arrived.

"Oh, no need to stop on account of me."

"Yes, Right Hand," Charlotte replied, although she didn't sit down and reopen the book.

Riley kept from smiling, knowing that the woman was giving her utmost respect to Riley's position.

"May I enter?" Riley asked, offering the same respect back to the servant. It was her job to monitor the comings and goings at this hour, and Riley would not presume to simply enter without permission.

"Yes, Right Hand. Assistant Prefect Mason is waiting for you."

"Thank you," Riley answered.

She pushed the door open and stepped into the trappings of royalty.

A large plush couch was in front of a fire pit, although the fire was out. Paintings adorned the walls—portraits of Mason's family, and of famous battles fought.

Mason's bedroom was in the back, although the door was closed, as it always was when Riley entered. The two had known each other for fifteen years, and never once had Mason been anything but a gentleman. He wouldn't even show her a bed, especially at this late hour.

Mason stood at the window with his back to her and his hands folded in front of him. The moon was high above the city, and Riley could see through the window that New Perth was still awake. Candles burned in windows, and people moved to and fro from bars and restaurants.

"Did I wake you?" Mason asked.

"No, Your Grace. I was awake."

"I'm sorry for calling you here so late, but I've been thinking all day long."

"Your Grace never needs to apologize to me."

"Will you drop the 'Your Grace' stuff, please?" Mason requested, still not turning around. "You don't like Charlotte calling you 'Right Hand,' do you?"

Riley smiled. "Okay, Mason."

"That man today…I haven't been able to stop thinking about him. Father thinks he's crazy, but he just seemed so…confident." Mason asked, "Did it bother you?"

"What he said?"

"No, his confidence."

Riley understood this was why she'd been chosen as his Right Hand. It wasn't her ability with the sword, her speed, or even her temperament. It was because they were always in sync.

"Yeah," she responded. "It's stuck with me most of the day."

"Me too. I'm wondering if my dad made a mistake sending him away."

"I wouldn't mention that to William." Riley gave a slight smile. "He's likely to toss you off the Grand Bridge."

"No, I don't plan on mentioning it to him or to Dad, but I'd be failing in my duties if I didn't follow up on it. Dad has so much else going on that it's hard for him sometimes to understand who the crazies are versus who actually deserves our attention.

"He's a good man."

"Yes, but that doesn't make him perfect." Mason turned around finally and looked at his Right Hand. "Listen, that man should still be in the city. I want you to find him and see exactly what he's talking about. There wasn't enough time at court today, so a lot of what he said sounded crazy, but that doesn't mean it was. It might just mean he didn't have time to explain it properly."

"Yes, Your Grace."

Mason shook his head, and Riley knew she'd made a mistake. "Okay, Mason."

"Don't tell anyone else what you're doing, okay? Just keep this between us for now."

"Of course," Riley replied. "Do you need me for anything else?"

"No, that's all. If something is brewing on the northern coast, we need to know about it."

Riley didn't sleep much that night. She didn't like to see Mason worrying; it made her worry more. Perhaps she dozed for an hour or so, but she was awake when the sun rose.

As soon as she saw it shining, she got out of bed. She didn't want to waste time when Mason assigned something to her, and if the sunlight was burning, then it was time for her to work.

She thought briefly about whether to wear her official garb or something that wouldn't identify her so readily. Since she was the Assistant Prefect's Right Hand, people would probably figure out who she was, but the purple robe would give her away immediately. Mason wanted this done as quietly as possible, so the robe was out of the question.

Riley dressed down, throwing on trousers and a simple shirt. She wouldn't be able to hide her sword from anyone, nor the adornments on the hilt. It would be at her side, and perhaps her hand could cover it some, but there wasn't a lot else she could do.

"Where are you off to?" William asked as she walked toward the stairs. Both Right Hands resided in the same wing, and their rooms were close to one another.

"Out." Riley stopped to face him for a moment.

"Dressed like that?" William asked.

"I know the people don't like you much, but they fawn over me, William. If I leave in my robe, I may never make it back. The crowds will be too large." Riley smiled as she spoke. She obviously wasn't going to tell William the truth, but he wasn't dumb. If she tried to lie, he'd ask more questions. If she joked, he might let her go without too much more pestering.

"You think you're cute, don't ya?" the big man asked.

"I only know I'm not as ugly as you, William." Riley smirked.

William grunted and closed his door.

Riley turned back to the stairs and started down them.

It took her a few minutes to exit the castle from the back. It was a massive structure, towering over the rest of New Perth. Riley knew she was lucky to live in it, especially since she came from a home that was more shack than house.

Riley knew the back paths to the castle well, though she doubted William did. When he left, he went through the main entrance, the double doors dwarfing even him in comparison. He would never try to sneak out the back, but Riley knew well that what she lacked in raw strength could be made up with speed and cunning—thus, always have more than one exit.

She quickly found herself in the market. People bustled around, the sound of vendors filling the streets, yelling about their produce and fish. Riley didn't pay it any mind, and no one was looking at her either. This was where she'd grown up, so the noises that might startle the royalty of the castle were only background to her.

She knew where she was heading. If anyone had an idea where the man from the court had gone, it would be Lucie.

Riley moved quickly through the streets, weaving in and out of people like water in a stream. The alehouse was on the corner at the end of the market. It was early in the morning, and while the market was busy, the alehouses weren't. Even drunks needed a break, which was why the market was so busy. Most of the restaurant proprietors were out getting their food for the rest of the day.

A large sign was over the door, simply reading LUCIE'S.

Riley pulled open the door and stepped inside.

The front room was empty, but Riley had expected that.

Lucie would be in the back, having already been to the market and gotten what she needed before the crowds showed up. Riley moved through the front room and pushed through the swinging door to the kitchen.

"Lucie?" she called.

"Oh, hell. Are you here to arrest me?" The voice came from the pantry in the back.

Riley smiled and started toward it. "Only if you don't give me what I want."

"That's extortion, which is illegal here in New Perth. I don't care whose hand you are and what they use you for."

Riley laughed at that, stepping into the pantry. Lucie was to the right, lifting a large bag of rice from the shelf. She was a short woman, but she had broad shoulders and a muscled back from years of doing what she was doing right now. Riley didn't even try to offer help. She'd probably be kicked out if she did.

Lucie was older, but she didn't look her age. Riley had no idea how old she actually was, only that it seemed like she had always been around. For most people in New Perth, she was as much a part of the kingdom as the castle.

Lucie lifted the bag with a small grunt and carried it past Riley into the kitchen. Riley quickly stepped out of her way, knowing she would be knocked over if she didn't.

The woman lugged the large bag to one of the counters as Riley followed her.

"How ya been over there in your glorious digs?"

"Trying to honor my boss," Riley answered.

"He a good one?" the woman asked, not looking up as she started loading rice into a large pot.

"He's better than I deserve," Riley told her with a smile.

"That's good. If he turns out to be anything less than that, you send Mason down to me, okay? I'll work out whatever is wrong with him right fast."

There were few people in New Perth who could speak in such a manner about the Assistant Prefect, but Lucie was one of them.

She finished adding the rice and turned around.

"Did Mason send you down here for food again? Because that's beneath you, and if he does it once more, I'm going to bring the food up there to him myself and let him know what I think."

"No, Lucie. He got that message loud and clear last time. He can't help it; he likes your cooking."

"Good." The woman nodded.

Riley wasn't sure Lucie knew how to smile; her face was a solid mask of sternness at all times. Riley had been scared of her when she was a child, but now she knew it was only a mask. A tough one, but a mask all the same.

"So what brings you down here if Assistant Prefect Mason has figured out how to get his own food?"

"A man came to court yesterday, and he was saying some...well, ridiculous things. Prefect Ire sent him away, but..." Her voice trailed off, not saying exactly what had transpired.

"But Mason wants you to look into it a bit more." Lucie turned around and grabbed the pot. She carried it a few feet to the sink, set it down, and started putting water in it. "This man...what's he saying?"

Riley felt relieved at the question. It meant Lucie was going to help, without directly saying so. Lucie had refused Riley before, and there wasn't anything she could do if that happened. She'd simply have to find another way.

"He said…" Riley shook her head. "You're not going to believe this, Lucie."

"Girl, do you want my help? If so, then give me the answers to the questions I'm askin'."

Riley nodded. "He said that farther north, up the coast, a man is holding people captive. He said sometimes they're held for years. The man is draining their magic and using it to increase his own. It sounds ludicrous, but that was what he said."

"Why would he want to drain magic from people?" Lucie asked, watching the water fill the large pot.

"I don't know. Prefect Ire kicked him out before he got the chance to say."

"But Mason thinks there's something to it?"

Riley was quiet.

"Fine. Do *you* think there's something to it?"

"I want to talk to him. He was…persistent." Riley wasn't going to go into detail about her and Mason's thoughts on it.

"If it were true, it would be one way to overtake Perth. No one has used magic here in decades. We are a truly magicless society."

"Magic can be dangerous," Riley answered.

"It can be, but it might be more dangerous that no one in New Perth knows how to use it. If what that man says is true, it would be very dangerous indeed. A sword can do a lot of damage and a cannonball even more, but a person who understands magic can dispatch both easily."

Riley wasn't going to argue with Lucie about that. No

one in New Perth used magic because everyone in New Perth believed it was dangerous. None of the previous Prefects had commanded that magic be banished. It was simply understood that to let loose such forces could be destructive. Peace was easier kept without it.

"I need to find him," Riley continued. "The man. Do you know where he is? Have you heard anything?"

"Might have. Might have been a man who didn't stop talking even after he got kicked out of the castle."

"Where is he?"

"Mac said he was giving him a room last night, but he didn't like it too much." Another grunt and Lucie lifted the filled pot, bringing it back to the stove. "Mac said the man sounded nuts and that he didn't have any money, but he'd give him a room for one night because... Well, mainly because Mac's balls are smaller than these grains of rice. He don't got the stones to kick a crazy man out into the streets, and that's why he hardly has the money to feed himself."

"Thanks, Lucie. I really appreciate it."

Lucie turned around. "Riley, I think you should be careful. You're quick as hell with that sword and you move as fast as anyone I've ever seen, but none of that matters as much as the pot behind me when it comes to magic. If what this man is saying is true you're gonna need help, girl."

Riley didn't like what Lucie had said. She didn't like the way the woman had looked at her. Lucie had known Riley when she was a child, moving through the streets just as quickly but picking pockets and purses. Lucie had been the one to pull Riley in and show her that there might be another kind of life for her if she wanted it.

Yet, in all the years she'd known Lucie, the woman had never told her to be careful.

Riley didn't have time to worry about it right now. She needed to report back to Mason, and Lucie had been railing about the lack of magic in New Perth for as long as Riley had known her. That wasn't going to change now, so of course she'd be concerned of rumors about an evil mage descending on the city.

Riley made her way to Mac's Lodge, although she had to rent a carriage for it. Mac's place was away from downtown, although it hadn't always been that way. Lucie hadn't been lying when she'd said Mac had a hard time turning people away, and although he'd once had a nicer lodge downtown, he wasn't able to afford the rent anymore.

Riley found Mac outside the building. His brother Miles and he were sitting at a small table playing a card game.

"And why do we deserve this visit from a Right Hand?" Mac asked, looking up with a smile across his large face. For every frown Lucie gave, Mac gave a smile.

If the two married they would probably kill each other, Riley thought, unable to help smiling back at Mac.

"Well, I'm hoping you can help me." Riley looked down at the game. Miles hadn't broken his concentration but was staring intensely at the cards before him.

"Did you get kicked out of the castle? Is that why you lack your fancy purple robe? Do you need a place to stay?"

"From the castle to Mac's Lodge. That would be appropriate, I guess," Riley mused.

"Besides the Prefect's castle, there is no finer lodging in New Perth."

Riley didn't dare look at the two-story building behind him. The two were joking now, but Mac was sensitive about his work. He cared a lot about it, and if his heart wasn't so big, he'd be a lot richer and have a grander building.

Riley switched her gaze from the game to Mac. "I spoke with Lucie this morning. She said you agreed to house a man last night, one who didn't have any currency and might have been saying some pretty odd things."

"Lucie told you that, aye?"

"She did."

"That woman has the loosest lips in New Perth." Mac shook his head though he kept smiling.

"How long have you known her, Mac?" Riley asked.

"Since I stood as high as your knees."

"Then you know she doesn't say a word that could hurt those she cares about."

"Maybe you're right," Mac said. "Anyway, yeah he's here. His name's Pat, and he's asking for a second night. I'm not gonna give it to 'im, though."

His brother snorted. "Right. Last time Mac kicked someone out of here I was probably as high as your knees too." Miles still didn't look up.

"New Perth has no heart anymore. I'm the last man in it with one. That's why when the Father and Mother return, I'm going to be first in line. Yeah, he's here, Riley. You wanting to talk to him?"

Riley nodded.

"I'm assuming this is official business?" Mac asked, his smile dying. "I can't just let anyone harass my customers, regardless of whether they're paying or not."

"It's not *official* official, but it's official enough, Mac."

The proprietor stared at her for a second, probably measuring whether he wanted to challenge a Right Hand.

"He's inside. Second floor. Room 46."

Mac looked back down at the game, clearly not happy with what he'd just done but apparently having decided that not *official* official was indeed official enough.

"Thanks, Mac."

Riley went through the lodge's front door. The stairs were to her right and she moved up them slowly, taking in the area around her. The man from yesterday had sounded crazy, and crazy created danger. While Riley could move quickly, she understood that to know your surroundings, you had to pay careful attention. She saw nothing out of the ordinary. No one standing in the main room downstairs. The bar was empty and the building quiet, for the most part.

She reached the second floor and found the correct door.

Standing to the side, Riley reached over and knocked hard. William would have handled this completely differently, but then again he was twice Riley's size and could afford to.

"Who is it?" someone called from inside.

Riley thought it was the man from yesterday, Pat, though his voice sounded more strained.

"My name is Riley Trident, and I represent the Assistant

Prefect. I'm here to speak with you about what you said in court yesterday."

There was silence on the other side for a few moments. "How do I know you're not lying?"

"If I were, why would I be knocking?"

More silence, and then Riley heard someone shuffling toward the door. It slowly cracked open, and Riley turned so that the person on the other side could see her. It was the man from yesterday, but Riley could see that he was nearing the breaking point. He believed what he had said yesterday, even if no one else in the world did.

"You threw me out," he whispered harshly.

"And now I'm here to talk to you about what you said. Would you like to tell me? Just you and me?"

He stared for a second longer, and Riley was sure he was deciding if this was a trick.

Finally, he opened the door.

"I'm leaving here anyway, so I guess it doesn't damn matter what you want to do. You can't keep me here, and I'm not staying." His words were rapid as he walked back into the small room. Riley looked down the short hallway that led to the bedroom but saw nothing dangerous.

It would be difficult to pull her sword out in this hallway if the man decided to do something, but she felt confident she could destroy him in hand to hand combat as well.

She followed him in and shut the door behind her. Pat sat down on the bed and Riley entered the room undisturbed. There was more room here, so she could free her sword easily.

Riley went to the window.

"I want you to tell me again what you told us yesterday," she demanded.

"I done told you all. I done told every one of you. You didn't wanna hear it, and so now I'm going to cross the desert and tell them. I'll go to Sidnie, because *he's* coming. He'll come here first, but next he's going *there*. That's the truth, and if you all won't listen, then maybe they will."

"I want to hear it," Riley persisted. The man had *really* pulled it together yesterday, because he looked to be coming unhinged. His hair was wild, a bird's nest of scraggly straw. His face was pale and waxy.

"It's what I told you yesterday. What I told your Prefect. He's got people in a compound, and he's using technology on them to pull their magic out. It's going to *him*. He's growing more powerful."

"All right," Riley responded. "I get that, but you've got to slow down. First, who is he?"

"I—I don't know."

Pat's back was to Riley and she shook her head, thinking herself stupid. This was a waste of time, but her duty required her to finish it.

"How did he find you, then?"

"You don't get it. That was years ago. He took me from Sidnie. That's where I'm from. Maybe he takes us all from there or maybe he doesn't, but how am I supposed to sit here on this bed and tell you how it happened? That's what you expect?"

"I expect you try," Riley demanded, her voice a steel whip from across the room. She was done wasting time with this delusional man if he couldn't get it together.

"I don't remember," Pat whispered, his head bowed.

"Things are comin' back slowly—certain things—but some stuff is just lost. That may be one of them. I don't remember how I got there."

Fine, Riley thought. *Just move on.*

"Where is it? Do you know?"

He nodded. "I do know that. I know exactly where that sonofabitch is."

"Where?"

"North. There's no city name. There's the ocean on one side and a forest on the other."

That describes almost half of the continent, Riley thought. "Could you take me there?"

The man turned around on the bed and looked at her. "Yes."

"How many people does he have?" Riley asked.

"I don't *know*. I wasn't privy to his accountin' for bodies," the man almost spat. "There were a lot. More than I could count when I was runnin'."

Riley ignored the hostility, focusing on the important parts of what the man was telling her. She needed to move the conversation forward. "How many days did it take you to travel here? Meaning, how long would it take us to get back?"

"I…" Pat looked away; Riley thought he was either trying to actually remember…or making something up. "I was sick. It's hard to remember. I slept a lot of the time in the beginnin', but if I had to guess, it'd take us ten days on foot."

Riley nodded. "I don't want you to leave New Perth. Wait here at Mac's for another day. I, or someone in my stead, will return with instructions tomorrow, okay?"

"Do you believe me?" Pat asked, his eyes finding Riley's again.

"I believe you believe it," Riley answered, her face hard.

He turned and looked back at his lap. "That's not enough."

"I found him. He's at Mac's."

"Mac Trolley?" Mason asked.

"The one and only." Riley grinned.

"What do you think?"

Mason and she stood in the castle's west garden. The sun was descending on the horizon, casting gold and orange hues across the land. Mason had been out here already when Riley returned. She'd changed into her purple robe, wanting to present herself correctly to the Assistant Prefect.

"I think the only way to really get the truth is to go up there with him."

Mason turned around, his eyebrows raised. "Go north?"

Riley nodded. "If he's lying, it's a perfect story. He was kidnapped and rendered useless for years. His memories of the time are nonexistent, for the most part. He only knows someone is behind everything, and that there's magic involved. But if he is lying, I should be able to find out pretty soon once I get up there. If he's not, then we need to know."

"Magic..." Mason's voice trailed off. "My father used to talk of it when I was younger. It was a big deal before he was Prefect, I think. He never gave me the details. I know they use it in Sidnie, and Dad says they use it on other continents too. He's never wanted it here, though, and neither did my grandfather. It's too risky, and the desert between Sidnie and us keeps it away."

He turned and looked at the flowers behind him, saying nothing.

Riley knew he was thinking. He'd always thought like this, his back to her, even when they were kids.

"I talked to Lucie today."

"What did she say?" Mason asked.

"She said to be careful. She didn't like the sound of what I told her—about magic being involved."

"That's what my dad doesn't see. New Perth doesn't use magic, even if the rest of the world does. We're isolated, though, and so it doesn't affect us. At least not yet. It could if someone wanted to use it against us."

"You've been reading up on the subject?" Riley smiled, teasing him.

"Actually, yes. It's my job to watch my father's blind spots, and one of them is magic."

"What would you have me do?" Riley's smile died away.

Mason turned around, his blue eyes finding hers.

I'd die for those eyes, she thought, and meant it. Those eyes had pulled her from the street and put her in this castle.

"I'm going to talk to Dad. You and William are going to go with this man and find out if what he's saying is the truth. Hopefully, it isn't. If it is, New Perth might be in trouble."

CHAPTER TWO

Rendal Hemmons' eyes were closed. His physical body was inside his compound, but mentally, he was far away. He was south. He was in New Perth.

He saw her clearly, the woman in the purple robe. She was thin and strong, with short hair which he felt sure had been cut to help her in battle. She was walking in a garden with young Mason Ire. Rendal knew his name and had seen him before, although not in person. Rendal had seen all of the Ires over many years because his magic connected easily with them. They had a long history together.

Even if the two alive now didn't know it.

But how could they? Rendal had been shunned all those years ago by Mason's grandfather.

She is perfect, he thought, looking at the Right Hand. *Her potential is unlimited, and she doesn't even know it. She is exactly what I need.*

Rendal had seen her before, of course. She'd been around Mason many, many times, and that was where he had first come to understand her potential. What she could do for him. He only needed to make sure he was ready, which he now was.

Riley.

The word rolled through his mind like a huge boulder, flattening everything.

She's perfect, he thought for the millionth time. And she was coming for him—*finally*. Rendal had gathered that much from the current conversation. Mason was sending her to discover the "escaped" man's truth.

It was all going according to plan. He would have this Right Hand and all her potential.

Every. Last. Bit.

Riley Trident was the reason Rendal had let Pat escape. She was the reason he let the man run south to New Perth. Because Rendal *wanted* Riley to come to him.

Rendal opened his eyes, dashing the vision away and coming back to the room.

Harold, his head guard, stood at Rendal's door.

"The new shipment is in, sir."

Rendal nodded. "Thank you, Harold. I'll be down shortly."

The new shipment. This one was late, and Rendal understood why. It was getting harder to find people and bring them from one side of this continent to the other. The cities on the east coast knew something was wrong, even if they couldn't say exactly what. It was an underlying knowledge that too many had gone missing over too many years.

Rendal and his soldiers had to be careful. Being caught kidnapping citizens from Sidnie, especially right now, might be the worst thing that could possibly happen. Rendal didn't want to battle Sidnie, only New Perth and the Prefect. At least right now. Eventually, though, Sidnie would fall too.

So the shipments were late.

And fewer.

And the people he needed for their magic growing less and less.

Heavy is the head that wears the crown, he thought, smiling a bit as he stood up. It would work out. It had so far, and just because things were tougher didn't mean they wouldn't go the way Rendal wanted. Especially now that she was coming—Riley. When she came for him, he would take her. She would give him a greater boost than all of the prisoners currently waiting for him below ground.

Rendal took the stairs up to the compound's surface.

A group of ten men and women stood shoulder to shoulder facing him. Their skin was deeply tanned from their travels. Dirt covered them, and they looked beyond exhausted.

"Welcome, friends." Rendal's guards moved away, giving him the room to walk where he wanted.

The prisoners were not bound by regular chains, but by green necklaces around their necks.

"I imagine you're all wondering why your magic isn't working here. I know in Sidnie, you all have free reign with magic. Perhaps you even asked some of my guards on the way, although I doubt they answered. You see, friends, what you have on your neck is a bit of technology I've developed over the years. I'm thinking about creating a brand name for it, maybe selling it in Sidnie. Something along the lines of 'Magitech' or 'Magience.' Get that one? Magic and science?"

He smiled.

"No, I didn't think it was that great either. I suppose I'll have to keep working at the marketing aspect. And truth be told, I didn't invent it. I've got a crackpot scientist working for me, but you probably aren't interested in him. Either way, the results are the same. You see the green lights on the necklaces wrapped around your brethren's necks? That's the technology at work, and it's limiting your ability to use your magic."

"Get fucked!" one of the women on the end shouted. "Our Prefect is probably already looking for us, and when he figures out where we are, you're a dead man!"

Rendal smiled wider.

"You Sidnie people always impress me with your gusto. Perhaps your Prefect *is* looking for me, but I doubt it. If he is, he won't pass through the Badlands over ten people. And either way, it won't matter soon."

"Let us loose, and you'll see what matters and what doesn't!" a man in the middle yelled.

Rendal shrugged. "Okay." He waved his hand in front of his chest and the green lights died away, the necklaces dropping to the ground.

The eyes of those in front of him glowed red.

Rendal's did the same.

Someone launched a fireball from his right. Without looking, Rendal simply raised his hand and pointed. Water droplets coalesced on the streaking fireball. They sizzled at first but grew more and more in number by the millisecond. The fireball vanished before reaching Rendal.

Rendal flashed a look at the man, and flames burst out on his body. He collapsed to the ground screaming.

"Who else would like a try?"

The woman on the left, the one who had screamed first, stepped up. Wind started to sweep around Rendal, picking up quickly. The woman was obviously adept at such magic.

"A noble try," he said as the wind tossed his hair and jostled his clothes.

He blew out, and the wind tossing harshly around him integrated his breath and coalesced into a thick, unseen force. It hit her in the chest, the hammer of air sending her skidding on her back across the ground.

The man wouldn't survive, but the woman would, and Rendal needed as many people as he could get.

He looked at the others, their glowing red eyes fading.

"Ah, you're seeing the truth of it now."

Rendal quit speaking for a moment, listening as the man groaned dying sobs on his right. The woman was slowly picking herself up off the ground, and she looked to have some broken ribs.

"This is your home now, friends. There are many Sidnians here already, so you're in good company. Guards, please take our guests below, and let's get them hooked up to our technology. It's time to start using them to their full potential, no?"

CHAPTER THREE

"I cannot *believe* you," William exclaimed.

Riley stood at her door staring at him.

"Did Prefect Ire tell you?"

"Yeah, he told me, and I'm fuckin' pissed," William replied. "I don't have time to go trekkin' north for some crazy man. I know this was your doing."

"It actually wasn't, William. This was Mason's idea. He thinks we need to check on it."

A day had passed since Riley had gone to see the crazy man, Pat. Mason was as good as his word, having gone to his father and gotten permission for the two Right Hands to travel north.

"We're expecting you back in nine days. The man said it would take ten on foot, but by horse, you should be able to get there in four," Mason had told her. "Four days there. Four days back. One day to look around. Make sure you're back in nine days, or we're going to think something is wrong."

Now, looking at William, she asked, "Are you packed?"

"Yeah, I'm packed. Are you ready, Riley? Because I'm not slowing down for you or the crazy man. I got three horses downstairs, and if either of you falls behind you're gonna be left. I'm getting north and then getting back, because this is all nonsense."

"Oh, calm down, chubby. There's no need for all this anger." Riley grinned as she stepped out of her room, enjoying seeing the big man all riled up. "Just think of it as a vacation."

"When I vacation, it won't be with you or the crazy man we're going to pick up."

"The crazy man and I are going to be a lot of fun. Just you wait and see."

"Fun as a damn disease," William retorted, though she saw a slight grin on his lips.

The two started heading toward the staircase, Riley intent on teasing William as much as she could on this trip. Riley had spent last night considering what they were doing. She still wasn't sure she believed Pat; there was a good chance the man was delusional. Yet, if he wasn't, between her and William, they could handle most anything that came their way.

They loaded their bags onto the horses. William's was a massive thoroughbred, necessary to hold the weight of the big man. His name was Broadsword. Riley's was much more like her, a lithe creature, and Riley thought her beyond beautiful. She'd named her Wind Whisper.

The third horse was for Pat, and not from the same stocks as the Right Hands'. Still, it was a solid, if nameless, horse.

It took an hour to get to Mac's, but both descended

from their horses and looked at the two brothers playing what appeared to be the same card game.

"Aye, Right Hand William Teller. How are you?" Mac stood up and put his hand forth. Mac had known Riley as a kid, but William had grown up in the castle.

"I didn't get that treatment yesterday," Riley teased.

"You need to grow another foot, lass, and then I'll stand for you too."

William shook the proprietor's hand, his own enveloping the smaller man's. Mac's brother neither stood nor looked up from the game.

"He still up there?" Riley asked.

"Sure is. Ain't left yet."

Riley looked at William. "Wait out here and let me go get him."

"Oh, no. We both know you're not strong enough to handle him alone. You'll need my help." He gave her a little wink as he looked away.

Riley chuckled, shook her head, and started inside. She was wearing her purple robe today, and would throughout their journey. This was official business, and the robe might help keep bandits and other ruffians at bay.

They marched upstairs, and just as Riley was about to knock on the door, William pushed by her, banging it open.

"Time to go!" he hollered roughly into the room, his bass voice echoing in the small chamber.

Pat was sitting on the bed, but he jumped up at the sound of the big man's voice. He stared at the giant, and Riley saw him actually start shaking.

"Hey, Pat, it's okay. William here has no manners, but

you can't blame him. Wolves raised him." She easily stepped between the big man and Pat. She smiled, trying to alleviate the tension. "We're here to head north. We're going to go check out what you told us."

Pat's eyes went from Riley to William and back to Riley.

"You serious?" he asked.

"Yes," William answered from behind her. "Get dressed."

A smile crossed Pat's face as tears filled his eyes.

He's either crazy or right, Riley thought, *because he believes this with all his heart.*

Given that Pat had almost no belongings, the three were downstairs in ten minutes.

"Look who showed up?" Mac commented. "Missus 'I Can't Keep My Mouth Closed.'"

"Maybe not mine, Mac, but if you don't keep yours closed, I can do it for ya."

Lucie stood next to the small table that the unending card game resided on. She didn't look at William or the man behind him. Her eyes were on Riley.

"You're goin' north?"

"Yes." Riley nodded as her eyes narrowed. This was unexpected, to say the least. Riley wasn't sure she'd ever seen Lucie outside her restaurant, except when she was at the market getting supplies. Yet here, in the middle of the day, she was standing at Mac's.

"I'm goin' too," she announced.

"The hell ya are," William grumbled. "I already have to

watch after these two. I damn sure ain't takin' no old woman."

Riley turned slightly, trying to stifle a wicked grin. "Chubby, you barely have the lung capacity to lace your boots."

She looked at Lucie.

"What are you talking about? You've got the restaurant to watch. There's no need for you to go north with us. How would you be able to help?"

Her questions were abundant because Lucie was making no sense. Riley couldn't even believe the woman was here now. Who was watching the restaurant?

"I'll worry 'bout my restaurant," Lucie quipped. "I'm goin' with you two, and that's all you need to concern yourselves with."

William started to say something, but Riley moved her hand down to her side, palm out and facing him in a "stop" gesture.

"Why, Lucie?"

That was the most important question. Riley had grown up around this woman. Indeed, it was Lucie who had first turned her from a life of crime and then introduced her to Mason, the man she now served tirelessly. She trusted Lucie implicitly, regardless of what William or anyone else might think.

"There might be things goin' on here that you don't know about, Riley. You either, ya big lug. If it's what I think it is, then I'm comin' along. If I don't, the chances of you two makin' it back are less than Mac here winnin' this card game."

Her face was hard because Lucie didn't care if she was

talking to the city's Right Hands or a street urchin. It was all the same to her. Humans were humans, regardless of what title they bestowed upon themselves.

"Okay," Riley responded.

"The hell?" William bellowed.

Riley turned to him whip-fast. "She'll be my responsibility. For all your blather about having to protect people, we both know I'll hold my own at least as well as you, so hush about that."

"And what about the Prefect? He hasn't given his permission."

"I'll take the blame if something happens." Riley wasn't giving in.

William must have seen the determination in Riley's face because he simply grunted and turned toward his horse. He grabbed Pat on the way, practically yanking him off his feet. Riley was kind and she was polite, but William knew the truth about her. He knew the steel that ran through her spine like those tracks they found sometimes out in the Wasteland.

She turned back to Lucie.

"You're going to need to tell me what you think is happening. I'll bring you along, but you can't keep it a secret."

"I'll tell ya, Riley, but not right now. I want to talk to that man over yonder for a bit. But before we get to where we're goin', I'll let you know what I think."

Riley stared at her, measuring the woman's words. There wasn't any lying in Lucie's character, and Riley sensed none now. Only a grim determination, and a feeling that something was very, very wrong.

CHAPTER FOUR

William rode in front, followed by Lucie, and then Pat. Riley took up the rear, and she kept a close eye on Pat. The man was quiet but fidgety. His eyes were constantly glancing at the surroundings as if he expected someone to simply appear out of nowhere.

The first day they rode without speaking much, the sun beating down harshly from above. They all sweated profusely, but William's clothes were soaked through, matted to his gigantic muscles. Each shoulder looked like a boulder next to his neck.

"Okay," he finally remarked as the sun dropped beneath the horizon. "We stop."

Riley looked around the area, scanning it quickly to see if there were any obvious issues. The road they traveled was little more than a dirt path stomped down by endless horses. Riley knew that the ocean waited to her left, but she couldn't see it from where she sat on her horse. To the right was dead yellow grass, and just a bit beyond that were the Badlands, an immense desert separating those who used magic from those who didn't.

A natural barrier, she thought. *It's kept us safe and allowed us to live without magic. But this man says that's not the case anymore.*

William swung off his horse and Riley thought she could see the beast sigh with relief.

"Come on, crazy man. Off."

Pat was still looking around, and Riley found herself growing more curious about him. He hadn't said a word the entire first day of travel, yet he was the reason they were heading north.

Riley helped make camp. There wasn't any wood to make a fire with, so as the sun set fully, the group was in darkness—only the moon lighting their campsite. Both Riley and William had brought provisions, Riley bringing extra for Pat.

Lucie had brought more than both of them combined.

"Did you pack anything besides food?" Riley asked.

"Hush, girl, 'less you don't want to eat."

And Riley hushed.

They had cheese and dried meat, and raisins and baked apples. There wasn't enough to stuff oneself, but Riley found she was surprisingly full.

"I'll take the first watch," William stated. "You're next, Riley. Are you going to survive on only four hours of sleep over the next few days?"

"If I remember correctly, your Right Hand test took place years and years ago. Mine was pretty recent." Riley smirked. "Are *you* going to be able to last on only four hours a night? I thought I saw you sleeping in the saddle today."

"When you see me sleeping in a saddle, I want you to give my broadsword here to the crazy man, okay?"

William didn't so much as look at Pat, only stood and walked into the distance. Riley watched him go, not concerned with him.

She wanted to talk to Lucie, and if Lucie was going to talk to Pat, then she wanted to hear it.

Time passed with no one saying anything. Riley wasn't going to rush it. Lucie had said she would speak when she was ready, and Lucie's word was enough.

Lucie unrolled a blanket and placed it on the dead grass, then laid down on it.

She closed her eyes. Riley didn't know if she was asleep, but she got the message clear enough.

Lucie wasn't saying anything tonight.

Riley rolled out her own blanket and laid down, turning her head to first Lucie and then Pat. The first day had been easy enough, although three more on little sleep wouldn't be a piece of cake despite what she'd told William.

She heard Pat lie down on his blanket. Her eyes automatically found her sword, the hilt within reach if need be.

An hour passed, with Riley falling deep into sleep.

"He's watching us."

The words snapped her from slumber, her arm reaching automatically for her blade. Finding the handle, she paused, listening.

There was no movement.

It'd only been Pat speaking.

He's watching us. Her mind recalled the words now that her instinct to defend was silent.

"Who?" She sat up, leaving her sword at her side.

"Him. The man who took me. The one we're going to."

Riley scanned the horizon in all directions. Her eyes were hawk-like, able to see almost as well at night as during the day. It was one of the reasons she'd been given the Right Hand. She found William still standing with his hand on his large sword.

"No," She laid back down. "There's no one here. You're just dreaming. I have to sleep, Pat. It's my watch in a few more hours."

"I can still feel him. It was the technology, I think. Whatever he hooked us up too. I think I'm still connected to him somehow, because he pulled my magic to him, and now it's living inside him."

Riley rolled over and looked across the campsite at Pat. He was lying on his side too, staring off into space.

"He sees us. He knows we're coming."

"And that's what you want, right? You want to go to him."

"Fuck yes, I do," Pat insisted. "It's *all* I want."

Riley kept watching him for a few more minutes, but the man said nothing else.

Since she'd met this strange man, she'd never heard so much steel in him. Those few words: *Fuck yes, I do. It's* all *I want.*

If this man does *exist,* Riley thought, *he's in a hell of a lot of trouble when Pat gets to him.*

"Bandits," William declared as he pulled his horse back.

Riley moved Wind Whisper to the left out of the line of horses so that she could see clearly.

Their small dirt path entered thick woods just ahead, and an hour ago when she first saw them, Riley couldn't have been happier. Shade would be a welcome relief from this unrelenting heat.

But now she saw the bandits, too. Or rather, Riley saw what they'd left behind. Things they hadn't thought anyone would notice, but her and William's eyes were far too sharp to miss them.

They'd done a good job of wiping their tracks as they moved into the woods, but they hadn't paid attention to the branches reaching out into the path. Perhaps there had been too many people, and they'd had to walk shoulder to shoulder on horseback. However it had happened, from thirty feet away, Riley could see the broken branches sticking out from the trees. They'd fallen to the ground and been kicked to the side by whoever cleaned up their tracks, but they hadn't bothered checking the branches still attached to the trees.

Although they probably couldn't have done much.

A broken branch was a broken branch.

"How long you think they been following us?" William slowly backed his horse toward hers, his voice low.

He stopped and hopped off Broadsword, then began rummaging through the horse's packs, all of it for show. Riley understood he didn't want the bandits to know they'd been spotted.

"I don't think they've been following us." She dismounted too. She spoke through lips that hardly moved, her voice soft. The Right Hand trained them to be covert if necessary. "I think they've got a lookout somewhere at the start of these forests. Probably using magnifying goggles. When they saw us, they cleaned up as best they could."

"Yeah. No way I didn't see 'em. No way. They must have seen us as far back as last night with them goggles."

"What do we do?" Pat asked.

"We go in there and kick their asses, that's what we do, crazy man."

Pat turned to the forest, and Riley looked at Lucie. The woman appeared no different than she had yesterday. Her face was stony and her demeanor unperturbed, a mountain that all weather would break against.

"You okay, Lucie?" Riley asked.

The woman nodded but said nothing.

"Okay." William ended the charade of searching his horse's bag. He pulled out a large jug of water, drank from it, and climbed back onto Broadsword. "You ready, skinny?"

"I'm ready, chubby." Riley hid the smile that wanted to dance across her mouth.

The four started into the forest.

The world grew dark around Riley, long shadows replacing bright sunlight. Her focus grew, her attention encompassing the world around her. Riley knew she and William could handle a lot, especially untrained bandits, but they also had to protect two people who couldn't defend themselves.

The path wove deeper and the branches above were thicker, the light growing less and less. Riley heard nothing besides the *clomp* of the horses stomping and insects chirping around them.

"It'll come soon." William's voice was a harsh whisper.

"Go ahead and dismount!"

William reined his horse in at the new voice, the line stopping. Riley's head whipped to her left and right, looking both high and low, but she saw nothing. Her sword had been unsheathed before the sentence was finished.

"You leave the two women, and we'll let you two men get outta here. You'll be on your feet, but it's better than not leaving at all, if ya know what I'm saying."

"How about you quit hiding behind the trees and get your ass out here?" William bellowed.

"Well, all right, if you insist," the voice responded, sounding like it came from everywhere at once.

Riley sensed the movement almost as it happened. Six men walked out of the forest. They were all heavily camou-flaged, even using face paint to help them blend in with the surrounding woods.

Three of the men held axes, the other three swords.

"Last chance, if you two gents want to hit the road. Of course, leave your horses, packs, and any other valuables. There's no need for us to fight. We'll take the ladies." The man in the middle spoke, and as he did, Riley saw his diseased gums and missing teeth.

"You can *take* whatever ya want." William swung his legs off his horse and landed with a *thud* on the ground. "But first ya gotta *get* it."

Riley slipped off Wind Whisper and silently moved to the other side of William's horse, quickly passing both Pat and Lucie.

"You can come take mine first," she remarked as she reached the front. "I promise that the first one to come only loses a limb. All the rest are going to die."

Riley hated people like this. When she was a kid stealing from people in the street, no one ever got hurt. Here, these able-bodied men weren't just stealing, they were raping and most likely murdering when it was over. This wasn't New Perth, but it was far too close.

"Oh, a sassy lady," the rotten-toothed man spat. "I like 'em with a little bit of fire."

"Then come get burned, prick," Riley rebuked.

The man moved forward, raising his axe in both hands. He took two steps and then started running, his mouth open in a horrific snarl.

Riley sidestepped to the left with ease, her sword slicing the man's right arm. His snarl turned to a scream as blood poured from his now-armless shoulder.

"You going to let me have any fun here?" William asked.

Riley turned back to the five men. They didn't appear to care at all about their fallen leader. Their eyes were still raw with anticipation.

"You want two or three?" Riley asked.

"You already got one?" William protested.

"You can count! I'm pleased."

"I bet I take four total."

"And I'll only get one more?" Riley asked. "I'll take that bet."

The five remaining bandits said nothing as the two Right Hands verbally jousted.

Then Riley moved. Her speed was almost supernatural,

her feet taking her across the dirt path to the three men on the right. Her sword reached out, its blade Death's touch. She danced through the men swinging axes and swords at her, running her point through their guts. Screams filled the air.

She felt the wind of an axe behind her and ducked quickly, then turned, bringing her sword up and catching the man beneath his chest plate.

Riley shoved him off her blade, and he collapsed to the ground.

All the bandits were dead or dying, their blood soaking the ground and their groans filling the forest.

"I got four," William declared.

Riley laughed, spinning to the big man. "The hell you did, chubby. The one behind me is mine, and these three right here are mine, too. Look at the size of the holes in them. That's my sword's work, not yours."

"Lies. These four here are mine."

Riley shook her head and looked at the two other travelers.

Pat's eyes were wide. "I've never seen anyone move as fast as you."

"She ain't that fast." William sheathed his sword and turned back to his horse. "The robe just makes her look like it."

Pat paid him no mind, and Riley felt a bit of blush moving to her face. She knew she was good—maybe better than good—but she didn't know how to handle being told that.

Ignoring Pat's stare, Riley went back to her horse and climbed on.

"Those four were mine." William pointed as their horses passed the dead bandits. "I don't care what you say."

The fire was dying, and Riley grabbed her blanket. She placed it on the ground and then walked over to Wind Whisper. The horse nickered at her approach, and she stroked his soft head. He moved his muzzle to her cheek, rubbing against her.

"That's a good boy," she crooned. "That's a good boy."

It wasn't the first death Wind Whisper had seen, but it'd been a while. He'd handled it well today. None of the horses had bucked or tried to run. She pulled a large carrot from the pocket of her trousers and let the horse take it in his strong jaws.

The purple robe was rolled up next to her blanket. She wasn't going to sleep in it, although it was more comfortable than these trousers.

"Fairly easy two days so far," William commented from his place by the fire. "Two more, and then I can get back to the castle. I tell you, crazy man, if we get there and find nothing, I'm going to ask that the Prefect put you in the stocks when we get back. And don't even *think* about running once we get there and discover this is all a lie. Riley here can catch you even if I can't, and wasting our time like this breaks a number of laws."

Riley patted Wind Whisper one more time and then walked back over to the campfire.

"Quit scaring him," she told William as she sat down. The night was starting to grow cold, and the fire felt good.

"I ain't scaring nobody. I'm telling him the truth."

Pat was staring at the fire, saying nothing. He'd calmed some today after Riley and William dispatched the bandits. Perhaps he hadn't believed the two Right Hands could handle what came their way, but the constant glancing around had slowed. He seemed to feel a bit safer, and Riley liked that.

Lucie still hadn't spoken much, and Riley *didn't* like that.

The woman hadn't laid her blanket down yet. She was sitting in front of the fire, staring at it the same as Pat. William had laid back and was resting his large hands on his stomach, watching the sky above him.

"You want first or second shift tonight?" he asked.

"Doesn't matter." Riley didn't take her eyes from Lucie.

"I'll take first, then. That's the main reason I'm putting crazy man here in the stocks. Because I'm losing sleep. A lot of it. Men my size, we need our rest. Takes more sleep to heal the day's activities, and this guy is just taking it all like it don't matter. As if I'm not losing valuable minutes full of sleep."

He smiled the whole time he spoke, amusing himself if no one else.

"Did you ever see this man?" Lucie asked, ignoring William. She didn't look up from the fire, but the question was clearly directed at Pat.

He looked at her.

"Yes," he replied quietly.

"Can you tell me what he looked like?"

Seconds passed in silence, the wood popping in the fire.

"He's tall. He's lean. Not emaciated so much as thin.

Kind of like Right Hand Riley, although not as…elegant. There's muscle to him. That's what I remember. He wears a black robe, but you can tell beneath it that he's ripped."

"His eyes—What color are they?" Lucie asked.

"A dull blue. Water beneath ice."

"Ain't that poetic?" William was still smiling. "'Water beneath ice.'"

"Hush, ya lout," Lucie lashed at him. She looked at Pat. "Don't mind him. He's not putting you in any stocks—"

"Am too." William laughed, clearly joking. Riley thought Pat believed him.

"I'd like to hear more about what happened to you," Lucie continued as if William had said nothing. "He had blue eyes? Pale blue?"

"Yeah, that's right," Pat nodded, his eyes sparkling now. Interested. Because he saw that someone believed him. Lucie might actually think the man was telling the truth.

"Did you ever see him use magic?"

Pat nodded, swallowing.

"Do you know anything about magic?" Lucie asked.

"I'm from Sidnie. Many of us use it. I could do it myself before I ended up there."

"What kind did you see him use?" Lucie continued.

"That's the thing—he don't classify what he does like we did in Sidnie. He uses them almost as one. I ain't never seen nothin' like it."

"What do you mean?" Riley asked. She knew almost nothing about magic; no one in New Perth did.

"Well, most people pick one kind of magic and they stick with it, ya know? Like you with that sword. You can prolly use other weapons, but the sword is whatcha like.

That's the way with magic. Other kinds are harder than the one you normally use, but him...he used them all."

Riley had heard of different types of magic, but she didn't know much more than that.

"Did you ever hear his name?" Lucie asked.

Pat shook his head. "No."

"Do you remember anything about how you were taken?" Lucie asked.

"I'm startin' to. There were others with me, I remember that now. I think it was early in the morning, and I think we'd been fishin' all night, bringing in a haul to sell at market."

"Was he there?"

"No. I would remember that without a doubt. I remember the first time I saw him, and it wasn't on that shore."

"The place we're headin'," Lucie said. "You say he's taking the magic potential from people and using it himself?"

Pat nodded again, and Riley found herself lost in the conversation between the two of them—completely enraptured.

"He talked a lot. He's arrogant. He 'splained it to us over the years. He said there are nanocytes in our blood, and that he was takin' them. He said he'd found a way to use them in his own body. I don't know, to be honest. Some people in Sidnie prolly understand all that stuff, but I was just a fisherman. I ain't ever learn anything about all that."

"Did he say how he was doing it?"

Pat shook his head. "Maybe. I don't know. I don't remember if he did."

Lucie stood and rolled her blanket out, seemingly done with the conversation.

"You all will believe anything." William stood. "I'm going on watch. Lucie, I always thought you were more level-headed than this, but you sound as nuts as crazy man over here." He shook his head and then walked off into the distance.

Riley watched him go, saying nothing.

She didn't bother putting the fire out. If it got out of control, William would catch it. Instead, she rolled her own blanket out and laid down.

Pat was the only one still sitting up, watching the fire.

"Lucie?" Riley began. "What's going on? What do you know?"

"I'm not sure yet, girl. I'll tell you when I'm more sure."

"Before we get there?" Riley asked. "Because we only have two more days."

"Yes, before then. Now get some sleep. I have a feelin' things are going to get tougher over the next couple of days. A lot tougher."

Pat remained up long after the two women had fallen asleep. He didn't sleep well anymore, or at least he hadn't since escaping. He didn't know if he would ever sleep well again.

The woman had asked him questions, the first person to do so since they had started this journey. The big man, William, didn't believe Pat at all. Pat didn't care. He didn't need anyone to believe him. They would see soon enough. In two days they'd all know the truth.

He wasn't sure if Riley believed him. He thought she wanted to, maybe, but what he said was too far out.

Again, it didn't matter. Soon, they'd see for themselves.

What concerned Pat was what they would do when they met the mage, because no one here practiced magic and Pat's ability to use his was gone. Maybe it would come back one day or maybe not, but either way, it certainly wouldn't return by the time they got to *him*.

True, he'd never seen anyone move like Riley had earlier in the day. She'd cut through those bandits as if they'd been no more than bags of sand, incapable of harming her. The big man could say he killed four all he wanted, but Pat had seen her move. She killed them in seconds flat.

William wasn't bad either. His brute strength was something regular men would flee. He swung his sword as hard as anyone Pat had ever seen.

But this mage wasn't a regular man.

They were bringing steel to fight someone who used magic.

New Perth didn't have what it would take to beat this man. Sidnie, perhaps. There were enough magic users there to stop the madman, but these two Right Hands were going to be massacred shortly. Pat had been dumb as hell to try to get them to come.

He stood up from his blanket and looked to where the big man stood. He'd been there for hours, unmoving, and soon he'd come wake Riley up to switch spots.

Pat started walking toward William, hoping the man didn't spook and shove his sword through Pat's guts.

"It's me. Don't kill me."

"I heard ya sit up." William smirked. "I knew you were comin' before you did."

The big man didn't turn around, and Pat had the distinct feeling that he didn't need to. If Pat were a danger, this giant could cut him down with hardly looking at him.

"What do you want, crazy man?"

Pat walked up next to him, stopping and looking into the distance. Pat had none of the night vision these two Right Hands did. To him, it all looked like darkness.

"I'm thinking we should turn around."

The big man's head turned, and he stared down at Pat. *Glowered* at him. "What?"

"I was wrong about this. I was all wrong. We need to go to Sidnie first. We have to get mages to come stop him. We can't do it."

William looked forward again, his sword strapped across his back. "You're scared?"

His voice was softer now, not the usual loud mocking tone, nor the anger from moments before.

"I'm gonna get us all killed. He's too powerful. We have swords, and he's got fire."

"It's okay to be scared," the big man responded. "There's no shame in that. Fear keeps us alive. It's kept me alive many a time. There *is* shame in letting it make you shirk your duty, though."

"My only duty is to get those people out. The ones still there. I know you don't believe it, but it's true. I'm going to get us all killed in two days."

"Maybe that's your duty, but it's not mine. My duty is to the Prefect, and he sent me up here to discover if what you're saying is the truth. I don't believe it, not for a second, but fear ain't gonna push me away from my duty."

"You'll die," Pat whispered. "He's far too powerful."

William nodded. "If you're right, maybe I will die. That's okay if it happens. A Right Hand *should* die if it's necessary. I'll be honest with you, crazy man. I don't see that happening. I'm good at what I do. I was the best until Riley back there came around, and I may still be the best, but she's quick on my heels. She'll pass me soon. She's dangerous, and one-on-one I'm not sure I could handle her. Whatever lies ahead, the two of us will go through it like shit through a kangaroo. She's not frightened, and neither am I. This is what we were made for, crazy man. To protect the Prefects, and kill people if necessary."

"You're not going to listen to me, are you?"

"I just did, crazy man. You just don't want to listen to *me*. There's nothing ahead that we can't handle, Riley and me. Now go get some sleep. I'll prove it to you in two days."

CHAPTER FIVE

The third day passed without incident. The ride was long and slow, the sun beating down as if it were angry at the Earth. Riley was quiet in the back, watching Lucie. Wondering if she was going to say anything to her or Pat.

Lucie remained quiet, and Pat said nothing either.

Only William seemed in good spirits, commenting as usual on what he was going to do to Pat when they returned to New Perth without having found anything of note. Riley knew the man was just boasting now, filling the time with talk. William didn't think anything lay ahead, and when they returned empty-handed, he would say nothing to the Prefect.

Finally, with the day ended, they dismounted their horses and made camp. Riley built a fire with deadfall from the forest while Lucie prepared their meal.

Riley kept her eyes on Pat since his unease appeared to be back. Perhaps even more so. He wasn't glancing around constantly, but he lived with fear—and it was growing worse.

They ate, and still the old woman said nothing. William seemed unconcerned, completely content with lying on his back and waiting until it was his turn to take the watch.

Pat stared at the fire.

Riley focused on Lucie.

"You going to tell us why you came all the way out here?" she finally asked. "Because tomorrow night we're going to reach the supposed compound, and I'd rather not hear about it an hour before if it's all the same to you."

It was the most directly she'd ever spoken to Lucie, but Riley was tired of being toyed with, and that's what this felt like. That the older woman was holding important information from them, despite having started this trip with the explicit direction that she would have to divulge it.

"I figured I would, yeah," Lucie answered. "Although I don't really want to."

"Oh, goodness, skinny." William's massive hands moved up and down on his stomach while he breathed. "Let it go. It don't matter what she says, just like it don't matter what crazy man over there says. We're going to be done with all this tomorrow."

Riley ignored him, but Pat was looking over now too.

"Do you know him?" Pat asked.

"Aye, I may. It was a long time ago, when New Perth was just bein' founded. The first Prefect wasn't even yet Prefect. That would be Goland's father."

"You were alive?" Riley asked, her eyes widening some. Lucie was old, true enough, but she didn't look *that* old.

"Aye, I was. It makes me wonder why Goland didn't see the truth in what this fellow is sayin'."

William let out a loud fart at that. "There's your truth."

"When New Perth was first being founded, Goland's father—his name was Simon. He was a strong man. A strong leader, and that was how he won."

"Won?" Riley asked.

"Yes. The Prefect position, but also New Perth's soul. He was in a struggle, though not a violent one. It was a struggle of wills, and Simon was strong. He was persuasive, and in the end, he got what he wanted."

"Which was what?"

"No magic, of course," Lucie told her. "Every once in a while someone might have an accident. The magic is in us, whether or not we want to acknowledge it, and sometimes it bubbles to the top without any help from us. Definitely in moments of stress, with people who hold a lot of potential it just pours out."

Riley said nothing. She gave no indication that she knew anything about that.

But you *do, don't you?* she thought. *You've never told anyone, but* you've *had* accidents.

"Simon thought magic was too dangerous, but he was a good man. He didn't want to command people not to use it. That would backfire. Instead, he used his pulpit to spread the message. To convince citizens of the dangers of magic, and that they should shun it. They taught their children that, and so on."

"We know all this," William retorted. "If you're going to give us a story, at least make it one we haven't heard."

"William, I just wish you had a brain the size of your big

toe. It's a damn shame ya don't." Lucie looked at Riley again. "What the steer doesn't know is that there was another man back then, too. Aye, New Perth did their best to wipe away his legacy, but he existed, no doubt about it."

Lucie paused for a moment. She moved her foot absently in the dirt, looking down at it.

"Most of our knowledge on this continent about magic comes from a woman named Linda. I never met her, but if the rumors are to be believed, she learned it from an old man with a beard and a staff in some far away land. I don't know the details, but I do know that Linda taught a group of people what she had learned; about 'Etheric energy' and 'nanocytes.' One of those was a man named Rendal. *He* thought humans should embrace magic. He thought it was our birthright after everything that happened before, and that magic would keep us safe and basically make sure we never wiped out the world again. Rendal Hemmons wanted us to use it; wanted everyone to use it."

"And this is the man we're supposedly going to hunt?" William asked.

"I think it might be."

"You know how damn silly you sound, Lucie?" William asked. "That man would be *old*. *You* would be old. Now I'm not sitting here saying you're a spring chicken, 'cause you're not, but you're certainly not *that* old."

"He would be old, that much is true. This would have been fifty or sixty years ago, and he was the same age as Simon. He probably would be ninety years old now."

"Exactly. That's not possible."

Pat shook his head. "No, that's not him. He's not that old."

"Let me finish, you two oafs. You don't want to believe me at the end, I don't give a rat's ass. Right now, though, I told Riley she'd know why I came, and that's what I intend on doing." Again, Lucie looked up from the fire at Riley. "When Simon won the hearts of New Perth, Rendal knew he was done. He could use magic back then. He *did* use magic, and the people of New Perth weren't going to have it. They...we... Well, we chased him out of the city. I'm not proud of that now, but we didn't hurt him. We just didn't want anything to do with magic back then, and he was the only one who could truly wield it."

"Where did he go?" Riley asked.

"I don't know. I thought he would make his way to Sidnie. It seemed like they went the opposite way of New Perth, embracing magic in a way we didn't. He could go there and feel free to use his powers any way he wanted. I thought he might try to get some kind of political power there, just as he'd done in New Perth, but I never heard of Rendal Hemmons again after that. Not until this man here came into the city talking."

"Lucie, all this ramblin' and you still can't tell me how this man is still alive. Crazy man here is finally having a moment of sense, saying that the man *isn't* that old. More, I want to know how old you are." William was having fun with this, his gruff voice filling the night air.

Riley knew the questions were legitimate, though. Things Lucie would have to answer if she actually wanted anyone to believe her.

"I don't know how he's alive," she responded simply. "I'm younger than Rendal by twenty years."

She glared at William.

"I don't want to hear nothin' 'bout me datin' someone that much older, either."

William grinned and avoided eye contact, looking like a much younger version of himself.

Lucie continued. "Goland is what…seventy or seventy-five years old right now? Mason is thirty? And Simon died ten years ago or so, although there wasn't much left of 'im by that point. I think if he's taking the Etheric energy from people, their magic basically, then he's somehow using it to keep himself alive."

"Ha!" William laughed. "That's less believable than the crazy man's story over here."

"I wish your ears were as big as your mouth is," Lucie snapped back. "Then you might be able to learn something. I'm not saying it *is* Rendal. I'm saying it might be. I'm saying if it is, then he's going to be pissed, and that's why all this is happening. We ran him out of New Perth, ya lout, after rejecting his ideas. If he didn't go to Sidnie, and he went north, he's been planning his return for sixty years."

Lucie turned back to the fire.

"He wanted magic to rule us, and mayhap he figured out a way to do just that. That's why I came—because I need to know if it's him."

Riley couldn't sleep much, and when William came to get her for her watch, she was already awake.

She looked around the campsite, but the other two were sleeping.

"What's keepin' ya up?" the big man asked. "Lucie's story?"

"Yeah." Riley stood and took her sword from the ground. "It's possible, whether or not you want to admit it, William."

"Aye, possible, but not likely. Someone would have told us."

"Who? Simon? She's right. The last ten years of his life, he was little more than a deranged man walking through the castle banging into walls. If Goland remembers, it surely didn't trigger anything when Pat came before the court. Mason wouldn't know anything about it. When we get back we can ask Goland, but right now we're on our own, and that makes me a bit nervous."

"Well, we'll see in just a few hours what's what," William retorted. "Now I'm gonna get some sleep. I hope you're rested enough to handle whatever comes our way."

She watched the big man descend onto his blanket.

I hope so, too, Riley thought.

She headed away from the campsite, her eyes adjusting to the darkness beyond the fire's embers.

Riley rarely doubted herself. Her skills with a sword were topnotch, and improving all the time. Yet what Lucie said had stuck with her all night.

A man exiled from his city and sent out into the wilderness. Even if he had made it to Sidnie, the Badlands separating New Perth and Sidnie were vast. He would have been lucky to survive at all. And if he hadn't gone? But instead turned north and began…

Began what? she wondered. *Kidnapping people from across the continent and sucking magic from their bodies, somehow able to funnel it into himself?*

It made no sense.

What Lucie had said about magic troubled Riley some, too. *Accidents.* Because Riley had experienced those before, and more than one. Many more than one. It happened when she grew overly stressed, although so far no one else had seen them. As a Right Hand Riley dealt with stress alone, never allowing the outside world to see any of it. Yet, hadn't she witnessed fire dancing across her fingertips? Hadn't she seen her eyes blazing red when staring in the mirror?

Yes, without a doubt. She'd never told a soul because New Perth didn't *use* magic. She was the Right Hand. She served royalty. She served *Mason.* To use magic...it would sully his family's name and destroy their relationship.

Yet Lucie had said it happened to other people, too. Those with a lot of potential.

What's that mean for me? Riley wondered.

She heard movement behind her and was on her feet with her sword drawn in a split second.

It was Pat. He stood over his blanket, not wanting to yell and risk waking everyone else up.

Riley waved him over, watching as he walked through the night.

"I just wanted to thank you," he said when he reached her. "I know you don't totally believe me, but you at least are giving me a chance to show everyone the truth. You're giving me a chance to rescue the people who are still there, still trapped. I wanted to thank you for that."

Riley nodded as the sky slowly grew lighter behind her. "It's my duty."

"Well, whatever happens tomorrow, I wanted to thank you."

Pat didn't move, however.

"There's more?" Riley asked.

"I—maybe," he answered. "The woman back there...Lucie. It feels like something is different about her. Do you feel it?"

Riley looked over the man's shoulder toward the campsite.

"I've known her my whole life, and I've always thought she was different. She took notice of me when no one else did, pulling me into her restaurant and giving me work when I was surely going to end up in the kingdom's stocks. No one else would have done that when I was a punk kid. So, yes, something *is* different about Lucie."

"That wasn't what I mean." Pat didn't look away.

Riley knew that. Something *was* different about Lucie, and for all Riley's awareness, she hadn't noticed it until tonight.

Not until she wanted you to, Riley thought. *Not until she finally opened up a bit about herself.*

"Maybe," was all she said to Pat, though. She turned back to him. "Look, we've got a couple more hours before the sun comes up and we finish this half of the journey. You need sleep."

Pat nodded. "Okay. Thanks again, Riley, or Right Hand, or whatever you want to be called."

He smiled, and it was the first time Riley had seen him do such a thing. It wasn't a horrible smile, either.

Dawn was almost upon the small group, and Lucie wasn't asleep despite what the people around her thought.

Lucie had told Riley most of what happened. She hadn't told her everything, though, and Lucie was struggling with that. Had she lied to the girl, or simply omitted certain things? And did it matter?

It matters, or you wouldn't be lyin' awake all night considerin' it.

That was the truth. Tomorrow (actually today, since the sun would poke above the horizon any minute), Lucie thought she would see Rendal again. It'd been a half-century or more, and Lucie had honestly thought he was gone forever. She'd hoped so. If she could be even more honest with herself, she'd hoped that Rendal had died.

Maybe on the way to Sidnie all those years ago, the Badlands taking him as it had others.

He's not dead, she thought. *It doesn't matter what William thinks, or Riley, or even Pat for that matter. You know the truth about Rendal, maybe better than anyone else ever did. He's not dead, and now he's returned.*

And then another thought came.

You're going to have to tell her. Tell Riley. You're goin' to have to tell William, too.

Lucie knew that was true, but she didn't want to. Those things happened decades ago, and Lucie thought she had outgrown them. She'd believed the past would remain in the past, and at the end of her life, she would have peace.

Lucie kept her eyes closed, but she knew Riley was standing guard thirty feet away or so.

But if he's returning, is it best that she's here?

Lucie had known since first laying eyes on the young girl that she was special. Riley didn't understand that, of course. She thought Lucie had simply been a kind old woman, taking her in when Riley was eleven. That wasn't the case, though—at least not all of it.

Riley carried potential. Not the kind most people spoke about—the potential to rise high in the world. She carried magical potential, and Lucie had seen her reaction when she mentioned "accidents." People becoming stressed and unable to hold their magic inside any longer.

It'd happened to Riley already, but then, Lucie had suspected as much.

That amount of potential... It wasn't really possible to avoid accidental magic flare-ups, especially if the girl got stressed. And as a Right Hand? There would be tremendous pressure on her almost all the time.

But what can you do? Lucie thought. *Simon was smart—very smart. He didn't outlaw magic, but rather made it so that it was shunned. The* people *decided against using it, and to use it now would invite ostracism. The city would turn against her, the Right Hand.*

Yet, laying in the wilderness, Lucie didn't think Riley would have a choice. If Rendal was alive, and this Pat is telling the truth, then New Perth might have no choice but to use magic.

All the steel in the world wouldn't matter against a mage.

Tomorrow, old woman, Lucie thought. *Tomorrow you will know for sure.*

CHAPTER SIX

Rendal knew the small group was approaching. They would arrive in the evening, and he wanted everything to be perfect when they did.

Harold stood behind him, having been called a few minutes earlier.

"Sir, how can I be of service?"

"Are you keeping up with our preparations?"

"Yes, sir. Everything is on schedule. Will they still arrive at the same time?"

Rendal had just projected himself to the trail the group was following and seen that their pace was the exact same. "Yes. They'll be here just as the sun goes down."

"We will be ready."

"You're sure, Harold?" Rendal asked. "I would sincerely hate for our guests to be disappointed with our effort."

"Yes, sir. Everything is in motion, and there will be no setbacks. It will be as you wish."

"Thank you, Harold. Your service is invaluable, as always."

"It's my pleasure, sir."

Rendal listened as Harold left the office.

Rendal wanted to be prepared for this evening as well. He stood from his chair and walked across his chamber, heading toward the door in the back. No one else used this room, let alone this door. There were a lot of precious things in Rendal's compound, but perhaps the most precious resided behind this singular door.

He pulled on the handle, and it opened easily beneath his touch. The room was a long one, like a walk-in closet except for what stood at the end.

It'd taken Rendal years of study to come to this understanding. After the World's Worst Day Ever, so much knowledge had been destroyed. And then the Age of Madness? Rendal had been *lucky* to meet Linda, lucky that she had met the man named Ezekiel. Linda had taught Rendal what he knew about magic—nanocytes and Etheric energy—but it was *he* who had dedicated himself to the technology in this room. He'd dedicated himself to finding an engineer who could build his ideas.

Linda was gone, but Rendal remained.

A chair sat at the end of the closet, a simple wooden thing.

Rendal walked to it, not bothering to shut the door behind him. No one would enter his chamber without being called.

Rendal sat down on the chair and rolled up his left sleeve. A circle of tiny scabs marched across the top of his wrist. He placed his left arm on the armrest and then, using his right, reached beneath it and pulled up the small clamp.

It was made of glass, and inside a dull green seemed to be waiting for something. Perhaps to be called upon.

Rendal tightened the clamp on his left wrist.

It would hurt a bit—it always did—but that was okay because pain was necessary. He wanted to be at his best tonight, and he needed more energy for that.

With his right hand, he pressed a small button on the chair, immediately feeling the needles poke into his wrist. The glass clamp lit up bright green as nanocytes flowed through it, moving from their holding container to his bloodstream. To their new master.

To Rendal.

He closed his eyes, the pain fading as his body began rejuvenating.

Whatever this group was bringing, he would be more than ready.

"Everything is prepared, Harold?"

"We are completely ready, sir."

"There's a fourth," Rendal commented. "How long has she been there?"

"We've been following them for three hours, sir. There have been four the entire time."

That's not possible, Rendal thought. *I've been watching them for days, and there have only been three. The two Right Hands and the man I let loose. There had been no fourth.*

He sent his mind out to the stranger, a woman who wore a hood. He tried to infiltrate her but ran up against a giant block, like a mountain cliff that refused to let him scale it.

That's not possible either.

Rendal was on top of his compound watching the strangers come.

"A change of plans, Harold, if you and your men can handle it."

"Yes, sir. How can I serve you?"

"I want you to send a group out to attack them. I want to see what they do."

"Now?" Harold asked with no hesitancy.

"Yes, now."

CHAPTER SEVEN

"Here they come." William pulled Broadsword's reins and brought the line to a halt.

Riley whipped her horse to the left, bringing him next to William. The other two remained behind the Right Hands.

"They've been watching us for hours." She knew that William had seen the signs too, though neither had said anything. "You starting to believe someone dangerous might be here, chubby?"

"Someone is definitely in that building." William stared at the structure. "But that don't mean it's a mage sucking the magic out of other people for nefarious purposes. Could just be a minor warlord. It ain't like they're not scattered among the Badlands."

The four had come out of the woods maybe three minutes ago, into an open space. There was a large building a thousand yards off.

A compound of sorts stood in front of them. It was four

stories high, and Riley could make out a few people standing atop it.

And now, people were coming for Riley's group.

Two large doors stood in the middle of the building's first floor. They'd opened, and seven people had rushed forward on horseback. They were riding hard, the horses' hooves kicking up dirt.

"Three bows, two axes, and two swords," William counted.

"I guess I'm going after the bows? You'd need to lose a hundred pounds before you'd have a chance of stopping them. Think you can do that in the two minutes before they get here?"

"Aye. You handle those three, and I'll make sure the other four die. I'm not sure how good your math is, but I've got more to deal with."

The seven started slowing down as they approached, bringing their horses to heel. They spread out slightly.

"You two get back," William grunted to Lucie and Pat.

"Oh, hi, cutie," a woman called from the middle. Her hair was short and scraggly, and one of her front teeth was missing. She looked like she might have once been a bandit, her skin deeply tanned and worn. She was looking behind Riley at Pat. "I remember you. Do you remember me?"

"He's not your concern anymore." Riley's voice carried across the distance. "We've been sent by Prefect Goland Ire to inspect these premises. We demand you put your weapons down, dismount, and move out of the way."

"Aye, do ya now? You demand it?" The woman looked

to her left and right. "She demands it, fellas. I guess we gotta do it, huh?"

"I got first dibs on her when she's disarmed," a man to the right declared. "You guys can have her after. I'll leave some to go around."

"Aye, you think so?" William reached to his back and brought his huge sword out from its sheath. "I think you might fit quite nicely on my sword when I shove it up your ass. What do you think, Riley? He big enough to fit on it?"

Riley pulled her sword, looking at the distance between the bows. These people obviously weren't well trained because to bring the bows this close was idiotic. They should have stayed back to pick off the strangers from a distance. Now they were within reach.

Damn it, Riley thought, knowing it would be easy to kill them, and William would still walk away with one more than her.

"Enough talk," the woman called. "Let's kill 'em."

The archers started trying to back up, realizing now how close they were. Riley wasted no time, spurring Wind Whisper and jetting across the short distance between the archers and her. She used her sword like a painter would a brush, her artwork death instead of canvas. The first she caught across the throat, and the second she impaled quickly through his guts. The third was a bit farther off, his horse picking up speed now.

"What're ya waiting for?" William hollered as he shoved two men off him. They flew into the air before falling to the ground and skidding across the dirt. "Get em!"

Wind Whisper charged across the open space. The

archer was slowing down now, reaching for an arrow from her quiver.

Hurry, Riley thought. *Hurry, or you're dead.*

The horse's hooves pounded the ground.

The archer nocked the arrow.

Two more seconds.

The archer pulled back the bow.

Riley's sword whipped through the air, although she was unsure if it would be in time.

The woman's scream answered her as blood poured down onto her saddle. She dropped the bow and fell to the ground, and Riley turned Wind Whisper to look back at William.

Three men lay on the ground, and he was staring at the crazy-looking woman.

"You want her?" he called.

The woman was trying to retreat, although Riley saw that she wasn't outright running. It would do no good since she was now on foot. Riley could run her down easily.

"I don't like beating on women. It's why *you* never catch a beating for all the mean things you say to me," William yelled across the expanse.

"First," Riley hollered back, "I'm never mean. And second, you couldn't lay a beating on me if the Prefect himself demanded it."

Riley and Wind Whisper crossed to William. The woman's horse had fled, and she was now looking at the dead skeptically.

"Let her go back in," Riley commanded.

"NO!" Pat shouted from behind, practically forgotten

by everyone. "No. Kill her. She's evil. She's as evil as the man inside there. I know her, and if you don't kill her you'll regret it!"

"We're within our rights." William was leaving the decision up to Riley.

"Let her go back in. One more isn't going to matter."

The woman turned her face to Riley, and in that instant, she regretted her decision.

"Ya dumb bitch. There's no forgiveness in this place, and you're going to learn that very soon."

The woman turned and ran, forgetting about her fallen comrades as well as her horse.

"That was stupid," Pat moaned. "That was so, so stupid."

Riley watched her go, wondering if she'd just made a mistake.

"I'm sorry, sir," Harold said. "I will send more."

"No, no," Rendal answered. "I just wanted to see what would happen. Nothing else. You did fine. Let them come now, and let's meet our guests properly. Please seat them, and I'll be down momentarily."

"Yes, sir."

Harold headed back into the building. Rendal stared at the four in the distance, two things going through his mind at once. First, he still didn't know who the fourth person was. The hood above their head blocked his view, and the mental wall blocked his mind. Whoever it was, they had somehow shielded themselves the entire trip.

No one from New Perth could do that. Perhaps there

were some in Sidnie, but none would dare cross the Badlands. The trip was too hard, and it'd taken Rendal many years and many soldiers lost to be able to do it consistently. Even now, he still lost men and prisoners during the treacherous trip.

No, this person had come from New Perth.

And there's only one person who could keep you out of their head, isn't there, Rendal?

It's possible, but she would be old, he told himself.

Still, it's possible.

He had Etheric energy, a constant supply of it. That was what kept him looking like this—using the energy to rejuvenate his cells.

She's not as old as you, though.

Plus, Rendal could think of no one else in New Perth who might be able to practice magic at a level that could keep him out of their heads.

Then it's her, and what of it? She made her choice long ago, and now she'll suffer the same fate as everyone else.

The second thought was about the young woman. Riley.

What he'd just seen had been brutally brilliant. She was a master of her craft, and her craft was killing.

Rendal was starting to see two paths available to him, and he wasn't sure which he wanted to take. He could, of course, just subdue her and throw her in the compound. He could take her Etheric energy as he did everyone else's, recycling it into his body—yet that would be somewhat fleeting. Removed from its host, the energy faded inside Rendal, leading him to need a constant supply. Given the amount of energy he imagined existed in her—the potential she possessed—hers would last a lot longer than anyone else Rendal had come across.

Yet, he saw a second option now.

Especially after watching her dispatch of the small army he'd sent down there. The woman had been ruthless against the three archers, dispatching them with a coldness and speed Rendal admired. True, she'd let the last woman go, but Rendal could work with that. He could teach her the power of callousness, the need to show no mercy, ever.

He could bring her into this. Into his revolution. He could show her the way, the future, and she could be his second-in-command. The two of them could take New Perth together, ruling like father and daughter.

Why commandeer her magic, if Rendal could simply command her? Yes, he wanted power...but he needn't have it *all* inside his own body. He could use her as she used her sword.

This young woman would have an option, the first Rendal ever granted anyone: she could serve him, or she could join him. Either way, he would possess her potential.

***

Riley and William led the group to the front doors.

"Do you believe yet?" Pat asked from behind.

"Like I said, crazy man, I believe we've got a warlord here, but he ain't stealing people and taking magic from 'em. That's not what's happenin' here. Sorry to break it to ya," William answered.

Riley was quiet, not wanting to get involved in their

quibble. The doors were opening again. Both of the Right Hands still held their swords.

"Welcome, ladies and gentlemen," a man spoke from the building's darkness. Riley peered through the open doors, hoping to see something, but the darkness was too complete. "My name is Harold, and I'll be your tour guide."

"And who are those dead people lying behind me?" William called. "They tour guides like you? Because if so, I'm happy to show myself around."

A chuckle came from the darkness, a light thing that didn't sound at all menacing.

"No, no. We only wanted to see what you were made of. We sent our least capable. The woman you let come back— she's a mutant from the Badlands, and I'm not entirely sure why we keep her around. You would have been doing me a favor by killing her."

"Why don't you bring yourself out here and let us get a gander atcha?" William called.

"Certainly, but would you mind putting your swords up first? I could overwhelm you with soldiers right now, despite your skill. Killing a hundred would be a lot different than killing seven, but I'd rather not do that. So, if you put your swords up, I can reveal myself and then we can continue with the tour."

Riley looked at William.

"What do you think, skinny?"

"I think we've seen enough to report back to Goland and Mason. Whatever is inside here, mage or just a man, he's too powerful and too close to New Perth for the Prefect to allow it to stand. There's no sense in going inside. It's dangerous."

William nodded, turning again to the blackness inside the open doors.

"Ya might be right, skinny, but I didn't come all this way to not know what the hell is inside there. Did you?"

Riley turned as well, still able to see nothing. She felt the weight of the sword in her hand, a comforting thing. No, she hadn't come all the way up here to be run off the moment they were faced with danger. She wanted to know what was inside so she could go back to Mason with actionable information.

"No. Let's go in."

"Good girl," William told her. "We're warriors, after all. Right Hands, and these people will bow to us. Go on and sheath your sword, but if they ask us to give 'em up we start cutting throats, okay?"

"You got it," Riley answered.

The two Right Hands shoved their swords into their sheaths.

"All right," William called. "Come on out so we can see you."

"Gladly."

A bright light flashed on inside the building, illuminating the whole area.

Riley struggled to keep her eyes from widening and showing her surprise.

She thought the voice they'd heard was coming from a small man—someone regal, who might be wearing glasses. Certainly someone educated better than Riley. The man before them looked like he'd seen more fighting than William or Riley.

He was large, almost as tall as William, and a bit wider.

An axe rested on his back, and a scar ran down his cheek to his neck.

"My name is Harold." The voice didn't fit the man before them at all. "I'm your tour guide."

William looked at Riley with his eyebrows raised. "Is this a joke?"

Riley shook her head. "I'm not sure." Keeping a straight face, she asked, "Harold, are you making a joke of some sort?"

"I assure you, ma'am, I am not." He looked past Riley to Pat. "Hello, Pat. Welcome home."

"Get fucked," Pat called. "This isn't my home."

Harold turned to Riley with a look that said, *What can you do?* "Are we ready to enter? My master is excited that you've come."

"Do you guarantee safe passage?" William asked.

"Guarantees? What guarantees are there in life? Come in, and let's look around. The master will decide what guarantees there may and may not be."

"Fuck it." William looked to Riley. "Ready?"

She nodded, still staring at the warrior who sounded like a professor.

"Where do we put our horses?" William asked.

"We have stables inside. Beneath. It's too hot to leave them out here, yes?"

Riley said nothing, only watched as Harold turned and started walking away. Riley spurred her horse but heard Pat say something behind her. She reined Wind Whisper in and looked over her shoulder.

"He sounds nice, you two," Pat spat. "He always sounds that way. I've seen him decapitate children. Don't trust him. He's a straight-out psychopath, loyal only to the master he talks about."

Riley looked at Lucie. The woman stared forward as if she were hearing nothing.

The four followed Harold into the building.

The horses were stabled, and Riley found herself staring in awe at the space. The room was huge, complete with hay and all the trappings of an actual stable. She'd never seen anything like it, and it was underground. The building stood four stories high, but so far they'd gone two stories beneath the ground. And there were even more underground floors.

Riley had seen nothing like what Pat described yet. No people in cages. No gruel being fed to them. No one with green necklaces on, having their magic stolen from their bodies. Their group hadn't even been disarmed. Riley's sword still hung from her side.

To Riley, for a place in the middle of nowhere, everything appeared relatively normal. She saw people coming and going through the hallways, all of them dressed like Harold in white robes. Some looked like they'd seen battle, and others looked like they lived in classrooms and probably didn't have a single callus on their hands.

"Here we are," Harold declared as the four walked into a large room.

A vast amount of food sat in front of them, enough to feed a party ten times their size. Riley had only seen feasts like this when the Prefect met with important dignitaries.

Her mouth opened and started to water. The smells were intoxicating. Roasted meat, grilled vegetables, fried bread, wine, milk. They even had iced water. As she scanned the table, the list went on and on, her body suddenly realizing how little nutrition it had had over the past few days.

"The master would like you to eat and regain your strength. The trip from New Perth to here is not a short one, and he realizes you must be hungry."

"Where is he?" William asked.

"He is here. He will come soon. It's him you want to meet, right? Pat told us he would be bringing people back, and we're happy he did. The master no longer wishes to hide in the northern regions, unknown. So eat, and he will join you shortly."

The big man bowed, oddly graceful for such a large person, then made his exit, leaving the four alone.

"Ah, hell," William said. "I'm gonna eat. I can fight on a full stomach."

He didn't waste any time but simply went to one end of the table and grabbed a plate. He started piling things high on it, and although Riley wanted to join him, the urge to understand what was happening right now was stronger. She didn't fault William for eating; she knew he was correct. If something happened that he didn't like, a lot of people in here were going to die.

Riley turned around and stared at Pat. The man was almost sheet-white.

"He knows who you are, I'll give you that. You also brought us here, which in itself says you weren't lying about *being* here. I'm not seeing the rest, though. The kidnapped people. The cages. This magic technology."

Pat only nodded. "You will. I told you both I made a mistake by bringing you. I told you both that we needed more people, and people with magic. It's too late now, though. You wouldn't listen."

Riley ignored him. His fear wasn't important now. She looked at Lucie. "Is this the guy? The one from fifty years ago?"

"I don't know yet," Lucie answered. She still had her hood up, which was odd, but her eyes were distant. She didn't look at Riley as she spoke, only stared over the banquet to the far wall. "I think we're going to find out soon."

"And what if it is?" Riley asked. "If it *is* him, what would you recommend we do?"

"I think we'll have to hear what he says," the old woman responded. "And then make our decision."

"Damn it." Riley turned back around. She walked across the room, grabbed a plate, and started angrily piling food onto it.

"You two are nearly worthless," William called. "Both of you claim to have met this man, and yet neither of you have any real advice. Crazy man here says we should run. Lucie says we need to wait. You see, skinny, you need to just listen to me. Eat your food, and then we'll see what's what. Stop asking them two questions."

Riley agreed with the big man but said nothing as she filled her plate. She sat down next to the other Right Hand and began eating. Pat and Lucie didn't move from their spots.

Riley was finishing her plate when she heard footsteps. She looked up quickly, her neck turning to the left where they were coming from. Seconds passed as the sound of someone walking grew louder.

And then the man was in the large doorway.

Riley stood with her hand on her sword. William only looked up from his plate, biting into a large turkey leg he held in both hands.

"Welcome." The stranger's voice was calm. He was tall like William but lanky like Riley. His face was hard, but not severely aged. He didn't look nearly as old as Lucie. Maybe in his fifties, but someone obviously still capable of physical feats.

His eyes.

Pat hadn't lied.

His eyes were that pale blue. A frozen lake.

"How is the food?"

"It's great." William ripped off another big bite. "Now, tell me why you sent out a group to kill the Prefect's Right Hands."

"Oh, that? We needed to make sure you were who your robes proclaimed you to be. If you were only impersonating a Right Hand... Well, we can't have bandits running around in here, can we?"

The man stepped farther into the room, his eyes moving from Riley and William to the others.

"Pat, how are you doing? I'm glad you've returned." His eyes fell on Lucie, but he said nothing.

The room froze as the two stared at each other. There was no doubt in Riley's mind that they knew each other.

"You hid from me." The tall man's voice was cold. "You were with them the whole time."

Lucie nodded.

"Why did you hide? Why did you block me?"

"That seems obvious, Rendal. I didn't want you to know I was coming."

The tall man stared for a moment longer and then looked back at Riley. "Sorry. Just some history that I was surprised to see entering the present. I was wondering if your Prefect would send someone when Pat here ran off."

Riley glanced at Pat, who was silent. He had moved closer to Lucie as if she could somehow protect him.

"Yeah," William grumbled, "and now we're here to look around. Pat here says you're plannin' an invasion of New Perth, and while I'm not buyin' everything he's saying, I don't appreciate being attacked when I walk up to a place. We're goin' to look around and decide for ourselves if there's a risk here."

"New Perth holds no sway in this place, Right Hand," the man responded. "I'm sure you know that. This is my property, not the Prefect's."

"Aye, I guess that sounds 'bout right." William took another bite. "But you should have thought about that before attackin' a Right Hand. It's akin to attackin' New Perth itself, so in a way, we're at war right now, you see? And unless you want this war to grow, you had best show me 'round."

William dropped the piece of meat he was eating and stood up from his chair.

"Do you understand what I'm gettin' at here?"

"I do," Rendal answered. "What would you like to see?"

Riley was still standing with her hand on her sword, not liking this at all. The man didn't seem nervous. It was as if he'd always planned on showing these Right Hands the inner workings of his operation.

"Crazy man," William called, "you're going to direct us. Show us where these cages are."

Pat swallowed, obviously not wanting to move.

Rendal smiled. "It's okay, Pat. You brought them here. Show them around. It will all be okay."

Riley walked across the room, turning her back on Rendal for the first time. She was trusting William to handle any possible attacks while she looked at Pat.

"This is why we came, right? Because we want to see if what you're saying is true. Now's your chance to show us it is."

"It's a trap," Pat whispered.

"That's fine," Riley answered. "We've been put in traps our whole way up here. We're good at getting out of them. If this is a trap, we'll get out of it too."

Pat nodded, although obviously still shaken.

"You," William called to Rendal. "I want you walking in front of everyone, including Pat. He'll lead us, and you just follow his directions. He says left, you go left, understand?"

"Of course." Rendal nodded. "That won't be a problem."

***

"I-I don't know where it is." Pat sounded lost.

They'd been walking for an hour, Pat calling out left and right and left and right. Riley didn't understand how it was possible that they were still winding through hallways.

They seemed endless, and she had no idea where they were headed.

Endless hallways beneath the ground at an already remote compound.

"Well, crazy man, we've been walkin' an awfully long time for you not to know where it is," William scolded. "And I'm tired of walkin'. I'm just plain tired, to be honest with ya, and you're the one who brought us up here."

Rendal turned around. "I wanted to let him show you around down here so that you can see he's... Well, he's lying to you. Now that you've seen it, perhaps we can venture up to ground level and discuss what's actually happening. Does that work?" He didn't look at Lucie as he spoke, only Riley and William.

"That sounds good to me," William answered.

"Come," Rendal told the group. "There's a quicker way upstairs than the winding one we just walked."

He wasn't lying. The walk back to the banquet hall took fifteen minutes, as opposed to the hour they'd just spent. Pat was relegated to the back of the line, behind even Lucie, while Riley questioned Rendal. Everything she'd seen up until this point, including Lucie's talk at the fire, had led her to believe what Pat was saying, yet they'd just been given a tour by Pat, and they'd seen nothing. Just hallways. They'd opened a few doors, the ones Pat directed them to, and each had been food storage.

"I'd like for just the three of us to talk if that's okay? You are official representatives of your government, and I am the ruler of this place, so it seems right."

"That works for us," William declared.

"If you'll come with me, Lucie and Pat can remain here.

I've had my servants prepare two tubs in the back of the room. They will find the water warm if they want to clean themselves."

"Don't leave." Pat's voice was only slightly above a whisper. "Don't leave me here."

Riley turned to Lucie. The old woman was acting stranger and stranger. Riley felt like she didn't know her at all. Lucie clearly knew Rendal, and he her, but nothing else made much sense. The man seemed almost regal, and protective toward the small part of the world he'd carved out. Yet, Lucie came here thinking it might be the man from her past, and he was—except Riley saw no magic. She saw no threat. Perhaps a warlord, and a powerful one, but nothing that could threaten New Perth. Certainly nothing that would have brought Lucie out of her restaurant.

Yet here she was.

"Are you okay?" Riley asked.

Lucie nodded.

"Can we leave you here?"

"We'll be fine, girl. Go see what Rendal has to say."

Riley nodded and turned back around. "They'll be safe? They might not be Right Hands, but they are New Perth citizens now, and if any harm befalls them, you'll answer to the Prefect."

"They're safe." Rendal smiled again. "As safe as you and your colleague here. Now, let's go upstairs to my quarters, and we can speak."

Rendal led them back to ground level and then to the fourth floor. The room they entered was glorious, even by the Prefect's standards. Overstuffed couches and chairs were everywhere. Tall floor-to-ceiling windows lined the walls, those on one side of the room looking out at the ocean, the other the forest.

"Come, sit." Rendal took his seat in a high backed chair.

William removed his sword and sat down on the couch. He laid the sword across his lap.

Riley remained standing next to the couch.

"Okay." William took the lead. "You tell me what's going on here. I've seen warlords, and this place ain't nothing like them. They live in huts out in the Badlands and squabble over sand. What you have here is a massive operation, tons of food, and actual warriors. A lot of 'em. The man downstairs might be crazy, because I don't see any cages or magic, but that doesn't mean this place is exactly friendly to New Perth."

"Pat worked here. The last few months, he started saying some of the things you're telling me now. Cages. Me stealing people's magical energy. It truly was crazy, and then one day he woke up and said he was leaving and bringing people back here. And, a few weeks later, here you are."

"Believable." William shrugged slightly. "Now what are you doin' up here? He worked for you? What'd he do for work, then?"

"I'm a merchant," Rendal answered. "All the food storage you see down there, it's arbitrage. I buy it at one price, and hold it until I can sell it at a higher price. Those tunnels and those storage rooms, they're what allow me to stay in business. It's cooler beneath the earth, naturally so, which helps keep my costs down."

"Who are you selling to?" William asked.

"Whoever. Warlords mainly. We run a good long-range

shipping business, as you can see from the docks out there. We have two ships there now, both of them from many miles away. Sometimes we sell to Sidnie if we have a serious arbitrage opportunity and can make it across the Badlands."

"Why don't you sell to New Perth?"

A sad smile spread across the man's face. "As I'm sure Lucie told you that I have a history with New Perth. I was once an important man there, even if no one knows my name now. I wasn't treated kindly on the way out, and if I've been forgotten, all the better. I'd rather *not* be remembered there, so I don't trade there."

As if Rendal weren't sitting in front of him, William looked at Riley. "I may actually put crazy man in the stocks. Four days of walkin' to hear *this*? What do ya think?"

Riley looked at the tall man sitting in his black robe with one leg crossed over the other.

"What happened there?" Riley asked. "On your wrist."

She saw tiny dots around his left wrist, which appeared to be scabs.

"Ah, that." Rendal glanced down without any display of nervousness. "I wear a bracelet sometimes, and while it looks beautiful, it's not very comfortable. Sometimes it grabs a little tighter than I'd like."

William was still looking at Riley, waiting for an answer.

"I'm okay with where things are," she finally responded.

"Good. Now we can get home."

"There's no need to run off today," Rendal replied. "I've prepared beds for you, and baths as well. You can each get a good night's sleep and begin your travel home tomorrow, but with more provisions. How does that sound?"

William studied the man, and Riley knew he was deciding whether to trust him. William didn't like this place, that was clear. He didn't like any place outside of New Perth and the Prefect's rule. This man could still be a danger to William and Riley. William simply didn't think him a danger to New Perth, which was why he was leaving. However, staying tonight might put the group at risk.

"How could I attack the Right Hand?" Rendal asked. "New Perth would fall on me like an avalanche. I would never survive."

William nodded. "You're smarter than you look if you know that to be true." He turned to Riley. "I'm okay with a night and provisions. Are you?"

Riley wasn't, but she nodded all the same. "Sure. A night sounds good."

CHAPTER EIGHT

Lucie walked through the hallways long after everyone else in her party had gone to sleep. The other three were exhausted, including the man who had escaped this place. Even with his outright terror at being here, Lucie knew sleep had come for him because she'd used magic to probe his mind.

When the three were asleep, she'd risen from her bed.

Rendal wasn't hiding from her, although he'd blocked off much of this compound. Lucie had been using magic all day to try to find out what was in here, but large areas were sealed off. Rendal had obviously used his magic to make sure that people couldn't see inside his operation.

Yet he wanted her to come to him now. That was why he wasn't hiding. She could see where he was, as well as how to get there.

The door was open, and Rendal sat with his back to her. He was close to the windows on the left, staring out at the night as the ocean beat against the shore. She stepped in.

"I was hoping you'd come."

"Your ability to persuade has grown stronger," Lucie responded. "It seems you've got the Right Hands eating out of yours."

"I was open and honest. That's why they trust me. I showed them around, and then gave them shelter and food."

"You didn't show them everything," Lucie chastised. "We both know that. What are you hiding here? Is it like Pat says?"

Rendal was quiet for a few moments, and when he spoke, it was as if Lucie had said nothing. "Do you ever wish you hadn't sided with the Prefect? That you had come with me?"

"No." Lucie shook her head.

"Why not? You still practice magic. You shielded yourself the entire way here, and even now you're trying to see the private places in my home. That was all I wanted. All we *both* wanted, really. That people could use magic."

"They weren't ready back then. That was what the city was telling you, and what you refused to hear. That was why they sided with Simon. But you wouldn't stop back then. You wouldn't just admit you'd lost. When people are ready to use magic, it'll come. There's no need to force it on 'em."

"You were wrong then, and you're wrong now, Lucie."

"Apparently not," she answered, "because New Perth is doing just fine without you, and I came to make sure that continues. Now tell me what you're doing here, and not the nonsense you peddled to the Right Hands. What are you hiding from me? What won't you let me see? Is it like Pat says? Are you somehow stealing people's magic?"

"Stealing. Theft. Those are strong words, Lucie. I don't like to consider myself in such a fashion. I'm bringing light to the world, and sometimes the light has to shine brighter for people to see it. Sometimes, it has to blaze."

Rendal stood up, turning so that he faced Lucie.

"I tried to bring light by myself, but it didn't work, did it? Even you sided with them, a *mage*." He shook his head in disgust. "So, now I'm going to bring a light they can't look away from."

Lucie knew then. Not everything. Not the details. But she knew that Pat hadn't been lying...and she knew something else too.

"You want her, don't you? The Right Hand. Riley."

Rendal smiled, the lights above casting shadows on his face. "You can feel her too?"

"Not her, Rendal. You stay away from her."

"Is she dear to you, Lucie? That's too bad, because I do want her, and over the years since I left New Perth, I've grown accustomed to getting what I want."

"Mayhap you did." Lucie glared at the mage. "But that's not happenin' now."

Her mind shot outward, searching for Riley's. She knew she'd startle the young woman badly, but there was no choice. They were all in grave danger.

GET UP, RILEY! she shouted directly into the Right Hand's mind. *GET UP AND RUN!*

Wind ripped from Rendal's open hand, knocking Lucie onto her side.

"I'd use fire, but I don't want to damage the room." Rendal smiled. "She will never escape here, Lucie. None of them will. They're mine, and New Perth will be too."

From the floor, Lucie watched as Rendal breathed outward from his lips. She maneuvered her hands, bringing up a field of dense air that surrounded her and took the impact. Even so, she was knocked back a few feet, although her magic took the brunt.

"Lucie, if you were ever a match for me, you're not now, my dear." Rendal gestured toward himself as if saying, *come.*

A massive armoire flew through the air as Lucie tried climbing to her feet. She saw it seconds before it slammed into her. She quickly threw up another air shield, slowing it some as she dodged to the right. The armoire clipped her hip and sent her sprawling to the floor again.

She looked around the room and saw him. Rendal Hemmons. The man she'd once loved. His eyes were alight with fire, and there was nothing left of the man she had known. There was only greed and the need to take.

"You're already dead, Rendal. Don't you see that?"

"No, Lucie. You just never started living."

He raised his hand, and with it, Lucie. She floated into the air, staring at him and not bothering to fight. She knew that Riley was moving, going to get William and Pat. With any luck, escaping this place. There was nothing Lucie could do now but hope.

"Come, I'll take you to the cages. There you can begin to understand what I'm building. You can even become a part of it."

Riley bolted out of bed, going directly for the sword that

lay to the side. She had it up and ready to kill before she even knew what was happening.

Her room was empty.

Her mind wasn't.

The voice was still echoing inside her head, although Riley had no idea how it was possible. She knew who was speaking to her, though, and no part of her denied it.

Lucie.

GET UP, RILEY! GET UP AND RUN!

Riley didn't bother to go for the purple robe that lay folded at the bottom of her bed, simply stepped out of the room and quietly closed the door behind her.

She heard footsteps from her right, just beyond the corner. Willam's room was two down on the left, near the corner where the guards would be in a second.

Riley said nothing, only trotted down the hall without making a sound, her sword at the ready. She leaned against the wall opposite William's door, waiting for the guards to reach her.

She heard their voices now, harsh whispers as the steps grew closer.

"He's a big motherfucker. It'll take all three of us. Just cut any piece of him you can."

"The bigger they are, the harder they fall. His fat ass is going to shake the entire building."

"Remember, don't touch the woman. Master wants her. She's not to be harmed."

"You think he'll let us have a piece when he's done?"

Then they were upon her. Riley wasted no time with talk. She danced through them, her sword her partner. It came and went, slicing limbs and piercing guts as if they were little more than air.

It took only a few seconds, and then she was standing on the other side of the hallway, four people lying dead or dying on the floor.

William's door opened, and a hand-axe flew through the air, smashing into the opposite wall.

"They're dead!" Riley shouted, not wanting William to rush out and attack her. "It's just me!"

He stepped through the doorway, his sword in front of him.

"You should tell me *before* I throw the axe! Where's the crazy man and Lucie?" His eyes were angry and a vein pulsed in his neck.

"I hope in their goddamn rooms."

William turned toward the rooms, but Riley stepped past him. "Stay here and watch. I'll get them."

She went first to Lucie's room, opening the door on the right. It was dark inside, but the candles from the main hallway shed some light. Riley saw no one inside. The room was empty.

"She's not here!"

"You can't trust old people!" William shouted back. "I knew she'd wander off!"

She stepped back out and then across the hall to Pat's room. She opened the door, flinging it back. Pat sat on the bed before her, his face pale and his hands on his lap. "He's coming for us, isn't he?"

"He's trying. Get up. We have to find Lucie and get out of here."

Pat stood. "There's no use trying. There's nothing we can do. He's too powerful."

"Ask the men lying in the hall how powerful he is. Let's go."

Riley went back into the hall.

"Anyone coming?" she called to William.

"Not yet, but if you move any slower, I'm sure they'll get here." William grinned.

Riley ignored him and rushed down the hall, Pat behind her.

"We have to find Lucie."

"We have to get out of here," William answered. "If we find her on the way that's fine, but our duty is to New Perth, not a restaurant owner."

Riley was so angry she wanted to spit fire. She couldn't imagine leaving Lucie in this place, but she knew William was right. Between Mason and Lucie, there was no choice. She served Mason, and she had to *live* in order to do that.

"Let's go," William grunted. He grabbed the hand-axe from the wall, shoving it into the strap on his boot.

The three of them wound through the halls. Riley was doing her best to remember how they'd gotten here, but it was hard. Every hallway looked the same, every corner a replica of the last.

"There they are!"

Riley whirled, seeing a group of four men staring at them from the other side of the hall.

"You ain't going nowhere. Go 'head put those weapons down. We'll make it easy on ya if you do. Easi*er*, at least."

"How about you come take them?" Riley yelled down the hall.

"Hard way, then. Fine by me."

The four men moved down the hall carefully. Riley could tell they were better trained than the others she'd come across.

"Move," William demanded from behind her.

She didn't waste time but spun her shoulders so that they both touched the wall. The hand-axe flew through the air, flipping end over end.

It caught the lead guard in the head, sending him to the floor. The remaining three looked down for a second but kept coming.

"What ya waiting on, skinny? Let's get 'em."

Riley moved then, sweeping down the hall like death's angel. She heard William behind her, his thundering footsteps echoing off the ceilings.

The first man met Riley's sword with his own, and the clanging of metal filled the air. Riley went low, but the man's sword was there already. She spun, bringing her sword up and then down in an arc aiming for the man's neck. His sword was there again.

"Here!" William shouted, reaching down to the hand-axe still stuck in the dead man. He popped it up into the air, and as Riley ducked the guard's swinging sword, she caught the axe in midair. Her momentum was moving in the right direction, and she didn't slow at all.

The hand-axe connected with the back of the man's knee. He screamed, and Riley thrust her sword into his stomach.

She tossed him to the side and William grabbed both of the other guards by their throats.

"One of you lives. One of you dies. You tell me who."

The men said nothing, only struggled to find air.

"Fine." William shrugged. He tossed the one on the left into the wall headfirst. He hit the concrete with a thud, blood splattering the wall and floor, and slumped.

"Okay," William spat, "you're the lucky one. You know what you're going to do? You're going to show us how to get the hell out of here right now."

The guard nodded, his face red.

William dropped him and he landed on all fours, breathing hard.

"How many more are coming?" William asked.

The man only coughed up spit.

"Do that again, and I'm going to kick you so hard your ribs end up in your throat. How many more of you are there?"

"We got orders to not let you leave," the man wheezed. "The whole compound is set on that."

"Great." Riley looked back down the other hall.

"I told you," Pat whispered. "We're not going anywhere."

Riley whirled on him. "That's enough. We're getting out of here, and I don't wanna hear any more shit from you about it. You think we're going to die, then go wait in your room for it to happen. Otherwise, grab that man's sword and help us hack our way out."

She didn't wait to see how Pat took it, only turned back to the guard still on his knees.

"You get up and start showing us where to go. Do it now." She placed her sword's point on his spine, letting him know what would happen if he didn't listen.

The guard got to his feet. His throat was purple, but he was otherwise unharmed.

"Listen to me well, prick," Riley commanded. "You're going to lead us *away* from your pals. Not to them. You take us to them, and you'll end up like your buddies on the ground. Got it?"

The guard nodded, clearly terrified.

"This way." He turned in the direction his now-dispatched group had come from.

The four ran. They moved quickly through the halls, always heading up. The minutes passed, and then Riley whispered harshly, "Stop. I hear guards."

William stepped up next to the guard leading them and held a knife from his belt to the man's throat. "Not a peep, unless you want a second smile across your neck."

The man gulped.

The voices grew louder for a second and then faded.

"Let's go."

The crew continued upward through the winding hallways.

"There. That's the door that'll let you out," the guard uttered.

"You're coming too, friend." William shoved him forward.

"No, no. I can't! I can't! He'll kill me if he knows I left!"

"You're walking out that door first." Riley moved her sword to the man's back. She and William were on the same wavelength. If people were waiting outside, they'd kill the first person who walked through.

She pressed the tip to the guard's back harder, and he went forward.

He pushed open the door, and for a second he was fine.

Then fire engulfed his body, and he stumbled forward, screaming.

The door closed, leaving them in silence.

"Well, we know we're not alone." William's eyes were still on the door.

"You're a genius. Have I ever told you that?" Riley asked.

"You should tell me that more. *Now* what are we goin' to do, skinny?"

She looked back down the hall they'd come from. There wasn't any escape that way; she was sure about that. Pat was next to useless now, even though he carried a sword. Riley turned back to the door. "We're going to have to get ourselves out of this mess."

"*Now* who's the genius?" William asked.

"You've got to go first, and it's not because I'm scared. You're bigger, and if anyone can take a direct blast of fire, it's you. I'll swoop around your side and start killing quickly. It'll hopefully distract them, and then you can bring your muscles down on them."

"That's convenient for you, skinny—letting me go first."

"It's the only way," she insisted.

"I know," the big man answered. He stepped forward, stretching himself to his full height. He looked massive in the cramped hallway. "Here we go. Make it fucking count."

Riley gripped her sword hard for a single second, simply to remind herself she carried it, then loosened her hand. It was easier to maneuver with a lazy grip, and she would have to use it like never before in the next few seconds.

William started running, and Riley was right behind him. He hit the door hard, springing out into the night air.

A fireball exploded immediately, and Riley couldn't tell what part of William it hit. She danced to her left, scoping out the scene as she moved. Ten guards, maybe more, stood in a semi-circle, with Rendal in the middle. His eyes were red, and Riley had heard what that meant. He *was* a mage, and that was where the fire was coming from.

"Try again!" William bellowed across the yard. He charged forward, his broadsword bared.

Riley moved to the left. The guards came for her, some screaming and others only grunting. She went through them silently, parrying blows and slicing her sword across soft body parts.

She heard William across the yard, his sword clanging against others. Grunts and screams filled the air as he killed the killers Rendal had sent for him.

"ENOUGH!"

The shout rose above everything, and Riley watched as the guards attacking her backpedaled at their master's call.

She turned to William. He now stood alone, two dead people at his feet, the rest having retreated.

He was bleeding and burnt. He would have scars, but he was alive.

Rendal stood in the middle, his eyes still red.

"It's you I want, Riley Trident," he told her. "If you stay with me, I will let the rest go. If you don't, I'll kill them, and you'll *still* stay. There's no way you're leaving now. No matter how hard you fight or how many of my men you kill, you're not leaving."

Rendal flicked his hand to the right and Riley watched as Lucie rushed through the air. She was floating and under the control of this master mage.

A glowing green necklace was around her neck, and her arms and legs were ramrod straight.

"If you stay, Lucie here will live. For a little while."

Riley was breathing hard, her eyes moving between William and Lucie.

"Don't listen to him," William called, his voice ragged. "You're not staying, Riley."

This was magic. This was what Riley had heard of but never seen—a power her sword couldn't attack. Fire and floating people, red eyes, and the ability to move objects with his mind. Riley's power rested in cold metal and ridiculously fast reflexes.

She was no match for this.

I either sacrifice myself, or I sacrifice them, she thought. *A sacrifice* will *be made to this mage, though.*

Riley thought of Mason. He had lifted her from a lifetime of poverty to the highest position she could ever want. If she were going to die here in front of this evil mage, what would make Mason proud?

"You want me? Come get me." She put her sword directly in front of her body, the point facing the sky. "Let's see if your magic can stop cold steel."

"Oh, you silly girl." Fire lit in his right hand as he flicked his left, sending Lucie floating back across the yard. He flung the fire out, but it spilled past Riley.

Slamming into Pat.

His screams rose into the sky, flames dancing across his body.

Riley didn't turn around to look at the dying man, even though her heart hurt for him. She had to stay focused. To glance away now would mean death for her, and William as well.

"That's one down," Rendal boasted. "Are you ready for the next?"

"I'm a Right Hand, you cretin. I serve royalty. You can kill as many as you want, but I won't bow to your will. But why don't we stop with all your threats, and you and I tango?"

"Have it your way," Rendal declared. "Guards, take care of her friend on my left."

Riley watched as Rendal rose into the air, seeing for the first time the bracelet on his wrist. It was the same glowing green as the necklace around Lucie's neck.

That's the technology Pat spoke of. Whatever that is, it's giving him power and allowing him to hold Lucie captive.

It was the last clear thought that went through Riley's mind.

Instinct took over.

Rendal's hands moved almost too quickly to see. Flecks of fire were flung from them, tiny arrowheads of flame. Riley moved, twisting left and right, dodging as best she could even as the fire reached out and singed her flesh.

She moved forward, spinning, ducking, and jumping. Always forward. Always trying to get closer to the mage. She barely heard William fighting, the sound of metal on metal almost disappearing as Riley fought her way closer.

Come, Riley. Come to me.

Rendal's words filled her head as Lucie's had earlier. Riley didn't understand it, and she didn't have time to think about it. She swung her sword to the right, slicing through a flock of fire and sending its small pieces scattering across the yard.

Good, good. Almost here, the mage said, his voice *inside* her mind.

And then she was in front of him, the fire gone, nothing separating Rendal from Riley's deadly steel.

She swept it down in a strong arc, aiming for his collarbone, intent on slicing right through the man.

Her arm stopped moving and she felt her feet lift off the ground, realizing that he had control of her as he had Lucie. The bracelet on his wrist was shining brightly in the darkness.

Riley was lifted into the air so that she was staring directly into his red eyes.

"Yes. You are perfect, my dear. Absolutely perfect." He looked to his left and Riley felt her head being turned to her right so that both of them stared at William. There were more dead around him, but four remained, and they were beating him back. Circling him, bringing their swords down on the huge man as he tried to parry.

"He's going to die," the mage insisted. "And you will watch. Then you will come back into the compound with me, just as I said you would."

The magic is in us whether or not we want to acknowledge it, and sometimes it bubbles to the top without any help from us. Definitely in moments of stress, and with people who hold a lot of potential. It just pours out.

Lucie's words fluttered through Riley's mind. She didn't know if they were from the past or something she said now, but as she stared at William, the words grew louder.

Definitely in moments of stress, and with people who hold a lot of potential. It just pours out.

DEFINITELY IN MOMENTS OF STRESS, AND WITH

PEOPLE WHO HOLD A LOT OF POTENTIAL. IT JUST POURS OUT.

IT JUST POURS OUT.

ITJUSTPOURSOUT.

Riley's eyes flickered to red, matching the evil mage's.

"Get fucked," she spat, and then Riley knew only the color red. It consumed her, and everything around her.

CHAPTER NINE

Riley remembered little of her travels back. She remembered the sun beating down constantly. Threatening to murder her and the man she traveled with. She remembered the man's weight; he was huge like a planet, unable to walk. She remembered tying the clothes of the dead together, creating a shitty sheet and strapping William to it. She remembered dragging him.

She remembered missing Wind Whisper, wanting her horse as badly as she wanted anything. There hadn't been time, though. She couldn't get to the horse.

Riley passed out sometimes, unable to hold her eyes open.

She slept sometimes, actually making camp.

Riley gave the big man water but took little for herself. She petted his hair at night, and between his feverish ravings, told him he was going to be okay.

She remembered always being on the lookout, confident that they were coming—the red-eyed mage and his minions. That they would find her and her friend and kill them both before she could make it back to New Perth.

Riley remembered little, but she continued on. The same steel that created her sword also made up her spine, and she didn't quit. Strapping the makeshift canvas to her back, she dragged the big man through the desert, woods, and ravines.

When Rendal's men came for her, she saw them a long distance away. She thought she might have been delirious, the riders on the horizon only figments in her mind. Yet, as she waited, the figures grew larger. That made sense, because why would they simply let her go? Why would they not send someone after her to finish the job that they started at Rendal's compound?

Riley set down the makeshift tarp, leaving the big man to lie groaning beneath the sun. She pulled her sword from its sheath and watched the seven riders come.

She remembered little of what came before in the travel, and she would remember little of what came next, but her mind returned to her at that point. The trained part that was pure killer. Righteous, but a killer all the same. She knew she might die as they approached. She was weak, and whatever had happened back at the mage's compound would not happen again. There would be no explosion from a well deep inside her.

Steel versus steel. That was how this would go, and perhaps she would lose. Either way, she would stand against them.

They descended from their horses and came for her, screaming.

Riley moved without thinking. She parried left and

right and spun like a deadly dancer listening to music that only she could hear.

Her sword slashed and cut. Screams and groans filled the air as blood fell to the ground.

One of their swords cut her left arm. Riley whipped around, catching the man across his throat. He dropped his weapon and dropped, trying to close the new hole with his hands.

In the end, the seven who had come for her on horseback lay on the ground around her. Their horses had long ago taken off, heading back to the compound. Riley hoped they would turn wild, not return to such an evil man.

She stared at the dead men for a moment, her chest heaving as breath surged in and out of her lungs.

There was nothing more to do except continue, so Riley grabbed the tarp and began pulling again.

More time passed, but she saw no other soldiers coming for her. Her mind retreated, the trained killer leaving and the lost and injured woman returning. She was on autopilot, trying to save herself and her friend.

At first, she thought the men were a mirage. She saw them in the distance, riding horses toward her. As they kept coming, she realized she wasn't hallucinating and unsheathed her sword, ready to fight again.

When she saw that their horses wore New Perth's emblem, Riley Trident, Right Hand of the Assistant Prefect, fell to her knees. Thin, sunburned, scratched, bleeding, and wounded, she knew that help had finally arrived. Mason had sent scouts.

The scouts placed both her and William on horses; one

rode with each, ensuring they didn't fall off. Riley went in and out of consciousness.

When they arrived at New Perth, she didn't hear the guards screaming down from the walls. The gates opened slowly after both the Prefect and Assistant Prefect were told of the happenings. Doctors and nurses rushed to the scene, and as the citizens tried to crowd around the Right Hands, they were thrown backward by soldiers, creating a wall of space between the wounded and the healthy.

The citizens wanted to see.

They'd heard the Right Hands were near death, and they had to see it—the most elite force in all of New Perth brought low by some unknown force.

They stared on as the doctors worked, moving out of the way when the Prefect and his son came. Mason rushed to Riley's side, not hearing any of the doctors' warnings that he might hurt her. He looked into her face, her eyes closed, and felt nothing but fear. His protector. His warrior. His Right Hand.

She lay before him unconscious.

"Will she live?" he called to the doctors.

"We don't know," came the answer.

Mason whirled to the man who had spoken. "She lives. Do you understand? She lives, or you'll be held responsible."

He'd never said anything like that before; never even thought such a thing. Yet, at that moment, all he cared about was Riley's life.

Riley living.

The Right Hands were finally transferred from the ground in front of New Perth to the castle's infirmary.

Mason didn't leave Riley's side, not even when the Right Hands were placed in different rooms. Not even when his father requested his attention. Mason did not leave.

Riley spoke once in the hours that followed.

She opened her eyes for a second, and Mason thought he saw recognition.

"Riley!" he practically yelled.

"He's coming," she whispered, her voice weak and raspy. "He's coming for me, and for New Perth."

CHAPTER TEN

Mason sat in front of his father, Goland. They were in the Prefect's private quarters, a place Mason was rarely invited to. He was the man's son, but there was a distance between them that he'd never been able to cross. Perhaps it was the death of Mason's mother during birth, or perhaps it was how Mason had taken to the streets instead of the court when he was young, but regardless, there was space separating them.

Physically and emotionally.

Mason's quarters were on the other side of the castle.

Mason's father rarely asked for his counsel.

Yet he'd been summoned.

Goland was seventy years old, and Mason thought this past year had been harder than the previous ones. His father moved slower. He spoke slower. Mason didn't know if that meant he thought slower, and he would never bring up such a thing. There might be a separation between the two, but Mason loved him and would serve him loyally until the man breathed his last.

Goland's head general, Verith, left the room as Mason entered, giving the Assistant Prefect a slight bow on his way out. Goland sat on the other side of the large living room. He had a cigarette in his hand, and Mason could tell he'd rolled it himself. He hardly smoked anymore, having given it up after the castle's head doctor said it was adding to his cough.

Sure enough, quitting had killed the cough.

But he was smoking now, the gray smoke floating up to the ceiling.

"I told Verith what Riley said." His father didn't stand.

Mason went to the chair the general had just given up but remained on his feet.

"Sit, sit," Goland said hurriedly.

"Yes, sir." Mason took his seat.

"You did a good job sending the scouts out to find them. Now, tell me again what Riley told you." His father was looking across the room, the ash long on his cigarette.

Mason nodded. "'He's coming. He's coming for me, and for New Perth.'"

Goland nodded. "That's what I thought. That's what I told Verith."

"What are you planning on doing?"

"She hasn't woken up yet, has she?" Goland asked as if he hadn't heard Mason's question.

"No, sir. Not yet. Neither has William."

"Twenty-four hours and they're both still out. What are the doctors saying?"

"It's touch and go. William was badly wounded. Multiple stab wounds and burns. They said he should have died during the attack, let alone made it the distance he did. Riley was physically hurt too, but not as badly. She's got a virus running through her, and the elements beat her down. They're trying to kill the virus, but her fever is worse this evening than it was yesterday."

"And the man they took with them? The one from the court?"

Mason shook his head. "There's no sign of him, sir."

"That's what I thought."

His father was silent for a moment, and Mason let him think.

"New Perth has never faced a true threat. We're prepared for one, or at least we think we are. We really won't know until it happens, though. That's when we'll understand if our preparations were worth a damn."

Mason nodded.

"The man, the one we can't find now—he was talking about magic in court that day, wasn't he? He was saying someone was using technology to steal people's magic and using it for themselves, right?"

"Yes, sir," Mason answered.

"I heard it, and I thought he was crazy. I thought he'd been in the sun too long, and I sent him on his way without considering it. Only when you came to me and asked that the Right Hands go check it out did I begin to think. Begin to consider."

"What, Father?"

The Prefect didn't look at him, just puffed slowly on the cigarette and stared at the wall.

"I was young. Twenty years old. My father was forty or so when the city granted him the title of Prefect. I didn't know what any of it meant back then, not really. I didn't know the responsibility that would come when the title passed to me. I loved my father, and I believed in his message. He had to keep a ragtag group of people together, help them survive after so much destruction.

"He had a rival, though. A man named Rendal Hemmons. Hemmons thought we should use magic. He thought it would make our lives easier; at least that's what he told people. My father never believed it, and neither did I. We both thought Rendal wanted everyone to use magic because he was the best at it. His skills far surpassed anyone else at that time, and if magic was used, he would be the most powerful man in the land. Hemmons wanted magic because it would create a caste system with him at the head.

"My father didn't want that and neither did I, and eventually the city sided with us. Hemmons tried to throw a coup, briefly. He was almost killed, and banned from the city. He never returned, and I honestly thought he'd died, son. I haven't thought of him in fifty years or so. When that man came to court, I never once thought about Rendal Hemmons."

His father paused, taking another drag. Mason had never heard of this Rendal Hemmons before. He'd known that his grandfather had been the city's first Prefect, but the opposing man had never been mentioned. He was never talked about.

"I went down to Lucie's restaurant early this morning before the sun came up so no one would recognize me. I wanted to ask her what she thought."

"Lucie?" Mason asked. "Why?"

"If I'm remembering correctly, she was Rendal's lover.

She used magic as well and sided with him when it came to what the city should do. Yet, when he lost and the people decided *not* to use magic, she obeyed their will. When Rendal's coup happened, she used her magic to help defeat and ban him, and as far as I know, she never used it again. I went to see if she thought it was him; was Rendal."

"Hold on. If they were my grandfather's age, how are they still alive?"

Goland nodded. "Rendal was my father's age. Lucie was younger than him. I thought it was an odd relationship, but I imagine their magic must have strengthened their love for each other. Lucie is old, but not *that* old. I don't know how Rendal is still alive."

Mason didn't know what to think and figured it didn't matter. They had to move forward. "What did Lucie say when you went to the restaurant?"

"She wasn't there."

"What?" Mason asked, nearly standing up from his chair. "She's *always* there. Lucie doesn't leave the restaurant."

"Someone else was there. He called himself a 'temporary manager.' He said Lucie had taken a vacation and should be back soon."

Mason stared down at the table, not fully understanding everything he was being told. Lucie was a mage? Lucie was missing? Lucie was some long lost mage's lover, who might also be coming to take down New Perth?

"This is a lot, Father. What are you saying?"

"A few things. One, William is burned. That means fire was involved, and mages use fire. They throw it like William does those hand-axes. Two, both of our Right

Hands were badly beaten in a trip to discover a mage. Three, Riley said he's coming for us." His father looked at him for the first time. "I'm not a genius, Mason, and I'm old. I'm not as quick as I was even ten years ago, let alone twenty, but I think it's Rendal. I think he's coming to claim the city he wanted for his own. I think he's bringing magic, too, and if so, we're in trouble. Our defenses will help, but are they going to be enough?"

"What do you need me to do, Father? I'm at your disposal."

"I know." Goland patted his son's hand. "It's a four-day trip, right? That's how long Riley told you it would take to get there?"

Mason nodded, feeling his father's hand on his for the first time in years. It felt odd, but also good. Yet, above everything else, it shoved the severity of this situation into sharp focus. His father would not show such emotion if death weren't drawing close.

"It will take you twice that to get to Sidnie, then another eight to get back. We're looking at over two weeks, but we need mages. If we're going to have a chance, we need magic."

"Then I'll go to Sidnie, Father." Another part of him thought of Riley. Of her still lying in the ward unconscious, and how he would have to leave her there.

The old man nodded. "Yes. Go today. Now. As soon as you leave this table. Without Riley, you'll need to take the Honor Guard. Take five of the best, and hurry, son. Move faster than you ever have before, because the city depends on it."

Everything was prepared, the Honor Guard waiting on Mason just outside the castle.

Mason knew duty propelled him forward; that he had to go to Sidnie or everything he loved would end. Yet, as the Guard waited on him, Mason wound his way to the castle's medical ward.

He went to Riley's bed and knelt next to her. He put her hand in his.

"I have to leave, Riley. Father is sending me to Sidnie because we have to have mages if we're going to stop what's coming. I'll be back, though. I'll return and I'll be right by your side again, although by then I'm sure you'll be walking around."

Tears were in his eyes as he stared at his Right Hand. He'd sent her north. He'd sent her with the man talking about magic and death, and now she lay unconscious with a fever ravaging her body.

"You have to get better, Riley. You have to come back to me. To New Perth. It needs you. *I* need you."

He stared at her for another few minutes, but his Right Hand did not move. She gave no indication that she knew he was there, and finally Mason stood.

He left the ward, heading toward the Badlands to find magic.

CHAPTER ELEVEN

Rendal's side was badly burned. Days later, and none of his magic had been able to speed up the healing process. His side was raw and painful. Only he and Lucie had survived the explosion in that yard; all his guards had been blown to bits. Well, Riley and the other Right Hand had also survived, but Rendal wasn't counting them. They were gone—escaped—and now Rendal was in severe pain, yet almost joyous at what he'd seen.

He was heading down to Lucie's prison. The prison levels were beneath the ground, of course, but Rendal had been kind to Lucie, giving her a cage all to herself.

Harold was with him, walking at his side. Rendal knew now that Harold would be discarded or severely demoted once Riley came into the fold. He was smart and capable with his weapons, but he was nothing compared to Riley Trident. He was an ant compared to her.

And why hadn't Harold been there when the Right Hand had exploded?

Something to deal with very soon, he thought as he entered Lucie's prison.

The room was extremely large, the ceiling fifty feet above Rendal's head. It'd taken years to get this place built to the correct dimensions. It all had to be perfect for his technology to work. Cages hung from the ceiling, some moving to different places. Rendal didn't concern himself with where the prisoners were going; he'd worked out the details long ago, and now it all functioned like a finely tuned clock. They would be fed. They would be cleaned. And then they would be *drained* of their energy.

A single cage was slowly being lowered from the high ceiling as Rendal limped across the floor. It took a minute or so, but eventually, Lucie was in front of him. The cage hung maybe a foot above the ground. She still wore the green necklace, both that and the cage keeping her from breaking out.

"You figured out how that works yet, Lucie? You were always smart."

The old woman said nothing, only stared at Rendal.

"I'm sure you know your magic is basically dead right now. All those people above you? They're mages too. Sidnie really embraced magic, like I wanted New Perth to do. It was a tough decision, stealing people from Sidnie. If they were to ever discover where I am, they could use magic against me, but New Perth can't. It would have been easier to simply steal you all, but then I might have been caught quicker. Plus, challenges bring out the best in people, don't you agree, Lucie?"

Only silence met his question.

"I'm sure you do. But me going to Sidnie meant I had to find some way to neutralize their magic, and that was when the necklace you now wear was born. You know how magic works. Your mind's focus, combined with your nanocytes and Etheric energy, allows you to interact with the world around you. To cross into people's minds. What I had to figure out was that it wasn't just your *mind's* focus that mattered. Your nanocytes have to be able to focus, too. They have to be able to listen to what you're telling them to do. That necklace stops that communication. Your nanocytes are constantly being scattered, like small dogs who can't look at any one thing for longer than a few moments. All the nanocytes in your body are like that right now, so although *you* may focus, they can't."

Rendal smiled, proud of himself. It was truly a feat of genius, how he'd figured it all out.

Lucie didn't seem impressed. "You are a bore, old man. I can't believe I ever went to bed with you."

Rendal ignored the slight. "How do you like what I've done with the place?"

"Did you come here to gloat about your insanity, Rendal? Is that the only reason you pulled me down?"

"Oh, no. Insanity didn't do this, my dear. Ambition did. A desire to finally see New Perth as it should always have been, a city on par with Sidnie as well as every other city on Irth. A city that embraces its full humanity instead of tossing half of it away like you all did. Like *you* did."

"I don't know why I ever loved you, Rendal. That man is long dead; I guess he died when he lost New Perth's heart all those years ago."

Rendal flipped his hand. "Enough. There's no need to dwell in the past. Did you see her? The Right Hand?"

Lucie looked skeptically at Rendal's bandaged side. "I think *you* saw her too, Rendal. Looks like you saw a bit too much. Maybe bit off more than you could chew, aye?"

"How long have you known she had that much potential?"

"Since I first saw her. She didn't even realize she was using magic back then. That was how strong she was."

"The things she can do, Lucie. The things I can do *with* her."

"Ha!" Lucie laughed. "She'll have no fucking part of ye, old man. That one is as honorable as they come, and if you go after her again, you'll find out in a much harsher fashion. Mayhap your whole body will end up in bandages."

Rendal blinked, staring at the woman. He didn't move, hardly even breathed.

And then he started laughing—loud, braying laughter that echoed off the ceilings and filled everyone's ears. He bent over, his side hurting, but unable to help himself.

Finally, after long moments, he straightened and looked at Lucie. "You don't get it, do you? Even after everything you're seeing here, you still don't get it." He shook his head and looked up. "All those people—why do you think they're here? Not as decorations. I'm taking the most important part of them and making it mine." He looked back down at Lucie. "The concentration of nanocytes in my bloodstream dwarfs anything you can imagine. What that girl did out in the yard was powerful for a mortal, Lucie. Yes. But I'm venturing into the world of immortality. I'm the most powerful mage ever to walk Irth, simply because of the sheer amount of energy I contain."

He cocked his head to the side, smiling.

"She may be powerful, but that's only to you. To me, she is another subject, one I think could be useful."

Lucie looked down at her feet, and Rendal thought she was finally seeing the truth: his power could not be contained nor thwarted.

When she looked up, though, Rendal knew that wasn't the case. The old woman was smiling.

"Heal up, Rendal. I can't wait for her to burn your ass to the core."

This would be a problem; Rendal couldn't deny it. Lucie stood in her cage and mocked him, but he didn't care about that. The issue was his side. It was badly burned, and he shouldn't even be up and moving around. His doctor had told him to remain in bed, and that exposing the flesh to air could easily cause infection.

Rendal didn't care about any of that. He supposed that he was helping himself heal *some* with magic, although not nearly as fast as he wanted. He *wanted* everything to be back to normal already, but that wasn't happening. Instead, he was fortifying his cells to keep infection at bay but wasn't quite able to rush the rest of the healing process. Or maybe he could if he simply did as the doctor asked and laid down.

It wouldn't be a bad idea, at least for a few hours.

Rendal went to his couch and pulled a pillow beneath his head.

This was what New Perth never saw. Healing magic like this. The ability to actually help cells regenerate, to support them so that people could live longer, healthier lives. They would see soon, though. Once Rendal had Riley, New Perth would see.

"Harold, we must talk," he told his guard.

Harold stepped farther into the room from his post at the door. Rendal knew how the man's loyalty was built; he'd been through Harold's head more times than he could count, and understood the intricacies of his personality. He was loyal to power, which was why he followed Rendal. Yet, the man hadn't been in the yard a few days ago when everything went down, and Rendal needed to understand why.

"Yes, sir. How can I be of service?"

"Before we get to that, Harold, let's talk about where you were when the woman decided to blow everyone up. You weren't in the yard. I was. Your second in command was. You weren't. Why?"

The guard didn't drop his eyes. "I was inside the building."

"I figured that, Harold. I didn't think you were standing in the woods watching us. *Why* were you in the *building?*"

"I was on the other side in case they came out there."

"The other side? The entire goal was to push them toward me, Harold. Not away from me."

"That's why I was there, sir. I was making sure that if they wound around the long way, they would find opposition. I was going to turn them and send them back toward you."

Rendal looked at his head guard, consciously shoving away the suspicion on his face. He reached out with his mind, sidestepping the man's words. He'd been silly to ask anyway. No one in this building could hide from him, which was why none of them had been taught to use magic. Rendal had spent years conquering warlords and enlisting their armies to his purpose. None knew magic, and none ever would. Rendal reigned over everyone's mind.

It only took a few seconds to discover the truth in the forefront of the man's mind.

It had been both. He had been ensuring that they didn't escape another way, but he was also scared of her.

A thought came. *Is he more scared of her than me? Because surely he would have known I'd ask this question. If he is, then his loyalty will flip.*

He looked through the man's mind quickly, but he couldn't find the answer to the question. He would need more time, because it wasn't at the forefront.

Rendal came back to reality. "Next time I want you by me. You send someone else to the other side of the compound. Do you understand?"

"Yes, sir. Of course."

Rendal nodded, turning his head on the pillow so that he was looking up at the ceiling.

"We are in a bit of a pickle here, and I have to figure out how to handle it."

I didn't expect her to escape, he thought, although he

wouldn't say that to Harold. If the man was questioning Rendal's power, that wouldn't help things much.

"I'm more injured than I expected, so I can't make my way to New Perth yet. The troops we sent to find her… they never returned?"

"Only their horses."

"So it's safe to say she killed them and most likely made it back to New Perth." Rendal felt calm about this; there was no anger running through him at the change in circumstances. Despite what Lucie had told him, he still felt confident in his plans. "After everything that's happened, how large an army can we muster if necessary?"

"I have a thousand men and women still under my command. Not all are at this compound, of course, but they can be summoned if necessary."

"No, no," Rendal said. "That won't be necessary."

A thousand men and women, he thought, *but that doesn't include my other plans.*

There *were* "other plans," although Rendal hadn't tested them yet. His engineer was still working on them, and that was something else to check on today. Time was speeding up now, the years of toil coming to fruition.

"I want you to take a group of soldiers to New Perth, Harold. That woman is important, and after seeing what she did there in the yard, I believe she's even more important than I originally thought. I want you to tell the old Prefect that I'll make him a deal. If he delivers the Right Hand to me, I will not fall upon New Perth. They can continue living their magicless life in peace, without worrying about me. If they do not give her to me, then they will live beneath my rule. Do you understand?"

"Sir," Harold said, "it may not be my place to ask, but is that the truth? If they give us the woman, we're going to leave them be?"

Rendal raised his hand to his head, closing his eyes and groaning. "No, Harold. It's not the fucking truth. I'm going to crush that city and remake it in my image whether or not they give me the woman. Stay focused, man. I want you to go down there, get her, and bring her back, and when we return, we'll burn the place."

<hr>

Side hurting, Rendal decided he wasn't leaving his suite. He'd have everyone come to *him* today. Usually, he preferred showing up at their place of work, especially Artino. The scientist was an idiosyncratic man who absolutely hated being interrupted, and Rendal got a real kick out of doing it.

He couldn't go down there today, though.

Harold had just left, and now he needed to know how his other bet was going. Rendal wasn't a simple man with only one plan. He'd learned that lesson back in New Perth. Then, his only plan had been to be voted in as Prefect, and when that hadn't happened, he'd quickly developed another plan.

It had failed, though.

And his second life had begun, sans everything he cared about.

Now Rendal knew he needed multiple paths to victory. The first was the energy in his blood.

The second was Artino's current work, deep in the

bowels of the compound.

The short man traveled upstairs and knocked on Rendal's door.

"Come in!" Rendal hoped the man would be perturbed. He'd given him no warning before summoning him.

"Yes, yes, I'm here." Artino walked through the doorway, his eyes on the floor. He started circling the floor immediately, not lifting his head. "You know I hate it when you interrupt me, Rendal. You *know* I do. I can't concentrate if I'm always being interrupted. I can't do my *work*, and let me remind you, it's not an *easy* task, what you've asked me to do."

He stopped talking and kept pacing his small figure eight across the floor.

Oh, Rendal loved it. He even forgot about his pain for a few moments. The man would pace like this for an hour or more if Rendal said nothing, lost in his thoughts.

Alas, there was no time.

"Calm down, Artino. It's going to be okay." He treated the man better than the rest of his underlings because the scientist was worth more. He was a positive genius. No one else on the continent could do what he was doing, or what he'd already done with draining energy from people. A genius had to be given a little leeway.

"Okay. Okay. What do you want, Rendal? Why did you call me up here?"

Rendal decided to fuck with him a bit more. "Do you not see I'm injured, Artino? Aren't you going to ask me how I'm doing?"

Artino stopped pacing and looked up. "So you are. I'm sorry. I hope you have a quick recovery." He couldn't hold the look for long and went back to pacing. "Now, what do you want? I have work to do. You know this. You gave me the work."

Rendal smiled and looked at the ceiling. "I just want to know how the work is going, Artino. I haven't checked on you in a while, and I know how you love our chats—"

"I do *not* love these, Rendal. I do not love them at all."

The smile on Rendal's face widened. "Anyway, I haven't been able to make it down there, so I wanted to hear your updates."

"We're close." He didn't look up and offered no other information.

"What's that mean, Artino?" Rendal swung his legs off the couch, sitting up despite the pain in his side.

"It means we're almost ready for a prototype."

"A prototype?"

"Yes. Yes. An experiment. A guinea pig."

"Guinea pig?" Rendal asked.

"It's a saying. We're almost ready to test it on someone. A live subject."

"Oh, that *is* good news, Artino. That is good news indeed. When will this happen?"

"It depends on whether you quit interrupting me. If you let me work properly, probably a week. If you continue these interruptions, these *constant* interruptions, then who knows, Rendal? Perhaps never."

Rendal hadn't seen the man in two weeks, so he found everything about this delightful.

"I'll let you get back to it, Artino. I'd like it ready in a week, though. Do you understand?"

Artino stopped pacing, hearing the change in Rendal's

voice—the deadly steel that so many others in this compound understood.

Rendal thought the man might piss his pants.

He smiled, releasing the tension. "Oh, don't take life so seriously, Artino. We're all going to die one day. Go on back to work."

Artino stared for a second longer, and Rendal felt the fear oozing off him.

That was good. He'd work harder.

CHAPTER TWELVE

We're not prepared for this, Mason thought.

There was no question why the desert had received the name "the Badlands." There was nothing good about it. No matter what direction Mason looked in, he saw only sand and sun. Sometimes, when he was lucky, he might see a sand tornado in the distance, which created variety.

If a dangerous kind. One of those could spring up at any moment right next to his party, and Mason didn't even want to consider what they would do then.

Four nights had come and gone since Mason left, and there were another four to go.

The horses were worse off than the men, but not by much. Mason was proud of his Honor Guard. None of them complained, and all kept their spines as straight as possible.

Yet, Mason knew the truth, because he was feeling it too.

The elements were killing them. There wasn't any other way to say it. Even with water and food, the sun was too hot and the distance too long.

That's not true, he thought. *We can make it. We* will *make it. New Perth needs us. Riley needs me.*

"Sir," the head of the Honor Guard spoke up. "There's something in the distance."

That man's name was Eisen, and while he would never fill Riley's shoes, Mason was coming to understand his competence. He ran his crew efficiently, everyone under him operating like a perfectly tuned machine.

Eisen had stopped his horse and was staring into the distance, one hand above his brow. The rest of the Guard had brought their horses up around his, all of them performing the exact same gesture as they peered forward.

"What is it?" Mason's horse remained behind the line they'd created. He didn't bother trying to see. His eyes weren't good enough, and he knew it. He'd met Riley as a kid when he'd tried his hand at pickpocketing. Lucie had caught him on his second or third attempt and told him, *You ain't never gonna be no good at that. You don't got the physical skills necessary. Stick to being a Prefect.*

She hadn't been lying. The men in front of him weren't just trained, they had also been chosen for a combination of physical skills. Their eyes saw farther than his now, and would into the future.

Riley was the best of them, he thought.

No, she is *the best of them. She's going to be fine.*

"A tent city."

"You're kidding." Mason could hardly believe it.

"I wish I was, sir," Eisen responded. "It's large."

Mason knew of tent cities. They existed throughout the Badlands. Sometimes warlords owned them, while others were more or less societal rejects. There were mutants in them, too—offspring of the nuclear explosion survivors, but their DNA had been altered. What Mason didn't know was how dangerous they were.

He had five men, which wasn't nearly enough to take down a tent city.

"How many people, Eisen?"

"It's tough to say, sir. I'd venture to say sixty to eighty." He asked his patrol, "Anyone think differently?"

"No, sir. That appears to be correct."

Mason nodded, thinking this through. The men in front of him were trained to protect with their bodies and kill if necessary. He was trained to lead, and through leading, protect those under him. That was what he had to do here.

"They've seen us?"

"Sir, I imagine they've seen us for days now. These tent city dwellers have eyes throughout the desert—eyes we can't necessarily see."

"If they've seen us and let us approach this far," Mason decided, "it most likely means they're not going to harm us until after they talk to us."

He looked at Eisen's horse and the pack on its flank. A New Perth flag was folded inside it. He could roll that out and display it as he went forward, but was it necessary? Their horses wore New Perth's royal purple, and that would be recognized even out here in the Badlands.

Displaying the flag might only show arrogance.

"Any other thoughts, Eisen, before I decide what we do?"

The man didn't turn around on his horse but kept gazing forward.

"Not a whole lot, sir. Whatever you decide, my men and I will surround you. I won't lie to you and say that we can definitely fight our way out. I've met tent people before, and they're a different lot. We'll be able to give 'em hell, and if they're untrained and weak, we'll be able to get to the other side."

Mason looked around the city to the left. They could skirt the side, perhaps lessening the chances of an altercation. It might not, though.

There were any number of things that could happen. Perhaps the tent people needed supplies. In that case, it wouldn't matter whether Mason and his team went forward. They'd be killed and robbed all the same. The tent people might have only let them this close so they wouldn't have to drag the loot very far.

Or they could be friendly-ish. Going to the side might be looked at as snubbing them. Like the people of New Perth were too good to speak to tent people.

Every choice had problems.

Riley's face came to Mason then. She always went forward, and she didn't skirt anything. That made up Mason's mind.

"Let's go forward."

"Yes, sir. Guard! I want a circle around the Assistant Prefect, and keep it tight! Nose to ass on every horse!"

Mason watched as the men reacted without question,

horses backing up and turning around until he was completely surrounded.

"Sir, I will set the pace, if that is permissible?"

"Yes. Let's go."

The group moved forward, a circle of horses with a bullseye in the middle. As they grew closer, Mason saw a group of tent people forming a straight line. They were all men, but behind them the women and children stood and watched. Their skin was a dark, dark tan and it was hard to tell what was dirt. It had to be there, living as they did in nothing but sand.

Eisen stopped his horse fifty feet in front of the line.

Mason looked over the tops of the Guards' heads. The tent people had no horses, and all held weapons of some sort. Swords, axes, and bow and arrows, all looking old and brittle.

They don't go to war often, Mason thought. *Those weapons won't hold up.*

More men were coming to the line, and there were at least twenty of them now.

"Eisen, I want you to move your horse and let me out, then accompany me to them."

"Sir, we don't even know if they speak our language. Tent people have their own dialects."

"Eisen," Mason said, "you heard what I told you?"

"Yes, sir. My apologies."

The man said nothing else, only spurred his horse forward, creating an opening in the circle. Mason trotted forward until his horse was parallel with Eisen's. "We go on foot."

Eisen gritted his teeth. "You know what your father will do to me if I let you get hurt?"

"Oh, I imagine it'll be better than what Riley will do to you." Mason grinned.

"So you're going to put me at risk with your father and your Right Hand?"

"Don't forget the people in front of us. I'm putting *you* in danger here too."

"True, Assistant Prefect. Days like today, I forget why I accepted this position."

Mason's smile broadened as he looked at the tent people. "Well, how else would you get to bask in my good looks and charm, Eisen?"

The guard's grimace broke then. "My apologies, sir. I have forgotten my whole purpose, which is to stare at your glory."

"There you go. That's the spirit. Just keep that in mind if these people decide to chop us up and feed us to vultures. You get to look at me as it happens."

Still grinning, both dismounted.

"Keep your sword sheathed unless it's necessary to pull it."

"Yes, sir," Eisen responded. Mason knew he sensed death in the air. Mason did too, but not right *now*. He sensed it in the future, after another four days in this unbearable heat. If bandits or tent people came upon them then? He and his men would be scattered like the grains of sand beneath their feet.

The two men walked forward and stopped ten feet from the line. Mason could see them well now. There *were* mutants here, showing physical deformities that had probably come down through multiple generations. Mason thought it likely the mutations stemmed from the World's Worst Day Ever, or slightly after the actual day. He'd heard of such things being caused by the weapons used, and the deformities were often passed from mother to child.

They didn't choose this life. They were run out.

"My name is Mason Ire, Assistant Prefect of New Perth. These men with me are my Honor Guard, and we all come in peace."

"Aye. Assistant Prefect, say ya?"

The man who spoke was bare-chested and had a deep tan like everyone else. A black tattoo of a rose sprawled across his chest. His head was bald, and he had a large gold hoop earring in his left ear. Mason saw two golden teeth sparkling from his mouth, both on top.

"Yes. May I ask your name?"

"I Worth. No last name. Tent people don't need last name."

"It's an honor to meet you, Worth. Are you this city's leader?"

"Aye. Hold the sword, don't I? Means I lead."

Mason saw the sword now, although he'd missed it before. It was across the man's back, and although Mason couldn't see the blade, he knew it was much larger than the other weapons the people held. Mason looked the man over but saw no physical deformities, and thus no reason for him to be out here.

"Why you here?" Worth's English was passable but rough, his accent strange to Mason's ears. It was like nothing he'd ever heard before.

"We're heading to Sidnie. We came across your city by

mistake, and we humbly apologize. Since we are here, though, I ask on my men's behalf if we can rest for a short time. No more than an hour."

"Rest, aye? Need water, betcha."

"We have our own water," Mason said. "My men only need to get out of the sun, and I'd like any advice you have for making it to Sidnie."

"Rest 'n advice, say ya."

The man turned his large head to the sky. "What say?"

Mason thought he was talking to the others around him, but he couldn't be sure.

"Aye."

"Aye."

"Aye."

The single word came up from multiple people, and then silence fell. The man remained staring at the sky for another moment. Finally, he looked at Mason again.

"Aye, they say. Aye, I say. Come. Your men rest. You, me talk. Aye?"

Mason nodded. "Yes, that's fine with me."

Mason needed an hour of sleep without the desert heat beating on him, but he had no choice in the matter. If this man wanted to speak, then he would have to speak.

He looked at Eisen. "I want you and the Guard to get a bit of sleep. I'm going to try to find out the easiest way to get to Sidnie."

"Sir, my men can sleep, but I cannot let you remain alone. I must stay with you."

Mason almost told him no, but saw immediately it wouldn't matter. Eisen wasn't going to sleep, even if it meant Mason removed his title for disobedience when they returned to New Perth.

"Fine. Tell them to rest. You and I'll talk with Worth."

Mason couldn't miss the deformities. He made sure not to stare, but to avoid them altogether would have perhaps been ruder. He would have had to look away from everyone he saw. There were tiny third legs attached to knees—things without bones, just flesh. Missing ears. Missing hands. Tongues split down the middle, which Mason thought might make communicating extremely tough.

The only person who wasn't obviously a mutant was Worth—a big, strong man, the rest of his tribe smaller and weaker. He walked with his back to Mason, showing no fear. The sword was long, at least as long as William's.

Eisen walked at Mason's side, his own sword sheathed.

Worth had given instructions to some of his tribe, and the rest of the Guard had been taken away to what appeared to be soft beds. The tent city was large, but Mason could see all the way across it. Everything was open right now, but apparently, drapes could be dropped both around the edges and in different places inside, creating rooms.

None dropped now, and he was thankful for it. The tent people weren't trying to hide anything from him, at least not from sight.

Worth sat down on a huge wooden chair, and Mason

had the distinct impression that no one else was allowed to sit on it. Only the man who carried the sword.

"There, there." Worth pointed to two bags in front of him. Grain bags, perhaps. Mason wasn't sure, but he sat down on one all the same. Eisen followed suit.

He looked at the bald man. His dialect was shabby, but Mason saw intelligence in his face. You had to be intelligent to live out here; there was no doubt about that. The dumb didn't survive in the Badlands.

He also saw a sense of humor, as if the bald man thought the whole world was a good-natured joke, despite the circumstances he lived in.

"Your men rest. You want advice. First, tell Worth why you go Sidnie."

Mason nodded.

"New Perth is going to be attacked by a mage. We don't practice magic in New Perth, but they do in Sidnie. We need help from them. We need mages, so I'm heading there to ask for their help."

"Hmmm." Worth put his hand to his bare chin and rubbed it roughly, almost angrily, as if he were trying to figure out a tough math problem but couldn't quite get there.

He's judging the truthfulness of my words, Mason thought.

"Mage who attack. Who he?"

"I don't know him," Mason answered. "He hurt someone close to me, my closest guard, and she said he's coming to conquer New Perth."

"Your Guard is woman?" Worth raised his eyebrows and looked at Eisen, shocked.

"No, no!" Mason smiled at Worth's meaning. "Not him.

No. He is a...a replacement. My closest guard was a woman."

Worth smiled at that, nodding. "I like. I like. Here, in tent city, all women can do all men work. All men can do all women work. 'Cept feeding baby. Men can't do that."

He laughed, and Mason realized he had made a joke at the end. Mason joined in, hoping to the Father and Mother that Eisen was laughing too.

"Too much judgment in world," Worth said when his laughter ended. "I like you let woman be guard. Aye, I like lots."

Mason didn't know what to say, so he kept quiet.

"Sidnie help, you think?"

"I don't know. I hope so."

"Magic, aye." Worth rubbed his hand on his chin again, more softly this time. He was silent for a moment, and then looked at Mason. "What kind magic you want?"

"I don't know," Mason said again, and truthfully. "I've never used it. I've never been trained in it."

"Look at us," the man responded. "Look close. Now."

Mason saw he meant it, wanting the Assistant Prefect to study his people. Mason did. They were small, and if pressed, Mason would say weak. Not quite sickly, but close.

"How many tent cities you think?"

"Total?" Mason asked. "Like in all of the Badlands?"

The bald man nodded.

"I have no idea."

"Lots. Lots and Lots. Warlords. Bandits. Worse, too. Mmmhmm. Worse. How you think we survive? How you think they not take us?"

Mason looked at the big man. "No one ever comes here? You avoid being taken over because you don't come in contact with anyone?"

"Ha!" Worth laughed loudly, his voice spreading across the tent. "He think we no war. He think we hide. Ha!"

The man didn't sound angry, and Mason was glad for that. Eisen was deadly, but *Mason* wasn't, and he wouldn't be able to do anything if this man wanted a fight.

"You wrong, Assistant to the Prefect."

Mason didn't correct the man's mistaken title, and he thanked the Father and Mother that Eisen didn't either. His guard wasn't stupid, and that was worth ten strongmen.

"We war. We no hide."

Mason watched as the man's eyes lit up red, the black pupils disappearing. The sand next to him started to swirl and Eisen jumped to his feet, his sword already out. Mason stood and backed up, his eyes wide and his mouth open. Worth didn't move or even look at Eisen's brandished weapon. He stared at the swirling sand.

Mason looked too.

It wasn't twirling up, but down, creating a pipe into the earth. A few seconds passed, and then Mason heard something else.

Water, he thought. *That's water bubbling.*

And sure enough, that was what came to the surface. Crystal-clear water flowing across the sand.

"We magic." Worth smiled. "Now what kind you need?"

Mason stood in the sun with Eisen at his side. They were a hundred feet away from the edge of the tent city, with their backs to it.

"Eisen, I know you may not be used to this, but I talk my decisions out. My father doesn't. He keeps everything inside, and when he comes to a conclusion, he'll tell you. That's not how I work. I need you to talk to me about this."

"Yes, sir," the guard said.

"And I need you to tell me your honest thoughts. Don't sugarcoat anything, you understand? Iron sharpens iron, and minds sharpen minds."

"I understand, sir."

Mason nodded, staring out at the desert before him.

"This is harder than I imagined. It's harder on me, and it's harder on you and your men than I thought it would be. We're halfway there. There's a long half yet to go."

Eisen nodded. "Living in the desert is a skill, and traveling through it is even harder."

"Exactly. So my options are, I go forward to Sidnie. I beg them to help us, and then I travel all the way back across the desert and hope I'm in time. Or, I see what this man wants, promise it to him, and then bring them back. You see the problems in both these options?"

"Yes, sir. In the first option, we might die before we make it back, or we might not make it back before the attack occurs. In the second, well…" Eisen chuckled. "They don't exactly look like saviors."

"That's right. Maybe they can survive out here with their magic, warding off small-time bandits, but are they going to be able to fight off what's coming for us? That's the question."

"It's a tough decision, sir, and I have no answer. It is time versus quality."

Mason was quiet for a second, then asked, "Do you know my Right Hand?"

"Yes, sir. I know Right Hand Trident."

"She's better than me." Mason's eyes grew distant as he thought about her. "She's better than me in almost every way, and I'm trying to decide what *she* would do right now. Her whole life she's looked up to me, and she would die for me, without a doubt. Yet I'm trying to figure out what she would do, because she's smarter and stronger."

Eisen said nothing for a few moments.

"Sir, I don't pretend to know Right Hand Trident like you do, so forgive me if I'm out of line. However, the woman I know is no coward. She is brave. If she were here, I think she would take this group of ragtags and head back to New Perth, because she wouldn't miss a war on account of travel. I apologize if that's too forward."

Mason shook his head. "No need to apologize. You're right. Let's see what these tent people want and whether we can give it to them."

Riley might be in a coma, but she was still helping Mason.

"What we want? Aye, that the question?"

"Yes," Mason answered. "If you fight for us in this war, what do you want for payment?"

"Payment, aye." Worth's eyes narrowed and he studied Mason carefully. "That the question." Worth stood and turned his back to the two men, looking out across his tiny kingdom. "I ask, they fight. They no say no."

They won't say no if I ask them to fight for you, Mason's mind interpreted the sentence.

Like my own men. Like Riley.

"This mage. He bad, yes? He hurt your woman?"

Mason didn't know exactly what Worth meant by *your* woman, but this wasn't the time to explore the details of his and Riley's relationship. "Yes. He's bad, and he hurt her. He's coming for her."

"For *her*?" The man turned around. "Why? Say."

Mason shook his head. "I don't know. I don't know a lot. She said he's coming for her and New Perth."

The man nodded, a knowing look on his face that Mason didn't understand.

"I not like them." Worth pointed to the tent people. "I have no third leg, third eye, one ear. I whole."

Mason nodded.

"My father. My mother. They bring us here. My father. He whole. Was whole. My mother, like them. My sister, like them. Me whole, like father."

"People came for my mother. My sister. Wanted kill. That why we here. That why I here. Because protect people we love, aye?"

"Aye," Mason whispered.

"You want protect this woman?"

"Aye," he whispered again.

"Payment." Worth brought his hand to his chin again. "What you say? *'I don't know,'* aye?"

Mason smiled. "Yes, I've said that a lot."

"I don't know," Worth answered. "You see how we do. You like, you pay, aye?"

Mason looked at Eisen, who only shrugged back.

"Sure. That works for me."

"Good, good, Assistant to the Prefect. That good. How many you need?"

"Mages?" Mason asked.

"We magic. How many you need?"

"How many can you spare?"

Worth looked at the tents, and despite his crude version of English, Mason thought the man was doing math. He was thinking about the children they had, and how many adults they could afford to lose permanently. What it would do to his city.

A minute passed, and Worth looked down at his feet.

"Five women. Five men. Plus me."

Mason leaned back on the bag of grain, considering. He'd left New Perth with no idea how many mages he needed. Now eleven were being volunteered.

Would that be enough?

Riley's voice spoke in his head.

He's coming for me, and for New Perth.

Ten would have to be enough because there wasn't any more time.

"Okay, we have a deal." Mason stood. "When can we leave?"

"On morrow." Worth finally turned around to face him. "You love her? Your woman?"

It was an odd question, and one Mason had never thought about. The tent person meant it in a different way than Mason was considering, or at least that was what

Mason believed. He thought Worth was asking about romance, but that wasn't what existed between Riley and him.

And yet he could only give one answer. "Yes."

The big man smiled broadly. "Good. Good. Love. Babies. We give magic. Kill mage. You marry. Have babies. Yes. Yes. This good."

CHAPTER THIRTEEN

Harold wasn't sure about his position any longer. He had been for a long, long time, since out of all the leaders Harold had known, Rendal was the most powerful.

Until this woman.

Now, Harold had begun to wonder if perhaps his horse was hitched to the wrong wagon.

"I gotta say, boss, I don't think this is the best idea."

Belarus—a man whose mere existence proved the Father and Mother did not care a whit about Harold. His second-in-command had been Leonard, a man Harold trusted. Unfortunately, the bitch Harold was now going to gather up had killed him when she blew up the whole damn yard.

And then his master—or "boss," as the idiot Belarus would surely say—had had the gall to ask Harold where he'd been.

Not there.

Not around that woman who was a killing machine.

He hadn't lied to Rendal; his intent had been to force

her back toward the main yard, but he had also wanted to fully understand her power. Harold was fine with having a master. Preferred one, actually. He just wanted to make sure his master was the most powerful, and he was starting to have doubts about that.

Belarus, for his part, continued talking as if Harold were actually listening.

"Going down to the biggest city this side of the continent and demanding they release someone we tried to kill? Well, it just seems to me like things could go wrong there."

"Does it now, Belarus?" Inside, Harold's temper was red-hot, but to the world, he remained as calm as the surface of a pond without wind.

Belarus nodded, his horse trotting beside Harold's.

He didn't want to think any more about the master or the problems there, so he decided to fuck with Belarus.

"What do you think might go wrong?"

"I mean, what if they say no?"

"Hmmm…" Harold feigned thought. "I'd never considered that. You think they might say no?"

"Yeah." Belarus's eyes lit up, thinking his boss was actually interested in his opinion. "Why would they just give her over, ya know? And if they don't, what do we do?"

Harold wanted to throw the man off his horse and stomp him to death with his own.

He didn't, though. Harold remained calm. "I'll give that some consideration, Belarus."

It bored him, fooling with this dimwitted soldier. He was little more than sword oil and hopefully would die in the first skirmish that arose. Two more days of this nonsense and they'd be in front of New Perth's gates.

"You think she's stronger than the boss?" Belarus piped up again.

Harold turned to the man, his head moving slowly because he couldn't really believe he had just heard that question.

Belarus was staring forward, riding as if he'd asked what the weather would be tomorrow.

Harold turned around as far as he could on his horse, looking to see who might have heard his new second-in-command. His troops were farther back, and thank the heavens for that.

Keeping his calm demeanor, he turned back to the path in front of them, the forest heavy on either side.

"Belarus, I would advise you to never say such a thing again. I'd advise you to never even think it."

Belarus raised his eyebrows. "Why? It's just you and me."

"Who do you think I report to?"

"The boss."

"That's right. The *boss*. How do you think he would deal with knowing that you're questioning his strength?"

Belarus swallowed, the click in his throat audible in the nearly silent woods.

"Exactly. The *boss* isn't going to deal with you doubting him in a very...gracious manner. And to answer your question, no, I don't think she's stronger than the *boss*. I think she's a good swordsman—"

"Swordswoman," Belarus interrupted.

"Thank you." Harold gritted his teeth. "Thank you for that correction. My *point*, dear Belarus, is that the woman is good with *swords*, but she doesn't possess what the *boss* does. She doesn't have magic like him."

"Then what happened in the yard?"

Harold thought it would be more fun to rub sandpaper over his eyeballs than continue talking to this imbecile. It wasn't that Harold disagreed with him necessarily. Hell, the woman was obviously something special. Even the master thought so. It was that this man was sitting there saying things that could get them *both* killed.

"Were you in the yard, Belarus?"

"Nuh-no…"

"Exactly. So how do you know what happened? You don't. You're conjecturing—"

"Conjectu-whatting?" Belarus interrupted again.

"You're making shit *up*." Harold's temper finally snapped. "You're making up *bullshit,* and asking me questions that I don't want to hear. The master is stronger. That bitch will either do what the master wants, or she'll die. That's all there is to it. Do you understand me? And speak clearly, because I want to know you mean it."

"I-I-I understand," he stuttered.

"Good. Now get back there with the rest of the men and keep your trap shut."

Belarus's horse slowed, leaving Harold to walk alone in the front. His head hurt, and he hated losing his temper like that. Not that he cared what the men thought about him. Belarus should fear him, and what had just happened would help instill that. No, Harold hated losing his temper because it was beneath him. It showed weakness if you let something rile you. The *inability* to keep yourself calm. Weakness could not be tolerated in him…or his master.

He sighed.

A horse sprang into view ahead.

Harold stopped, raising his hand to signal those behind him.

He waited, a minute passing, and then recognized the master's symbol on the oncoming horse. A glowing green band.

It was the scout, and he must have seen something or he wouldn't be returning.

"Sir." The rider and his horse approached. "There's a caravan up ahead about twenty miles. They're heading this way."

"How many people?" Harold asked. He knew what the men behind him would want, of course, but he had to keep the master's goal in mind.

"Appears to be thirty, best we can tell."

Harold nodded. He could almost feel the men's giddiness.

"They're in our path?"

"Yes, sir. We'll cross right over them."

Well, there wasn't anything he could do about that. He couldn't hold the men back if he wanted to if they would be running across a caravan most likely loaded with women *and* treasure of one kind or another.

"We'll take them."

Cheers rang behind him.

Harold didn't care. He just wanted to get down there to that bitch.

The master wanted her for his own purposes, but Harold was starting to think he might have run across someone more powerful than Rendal Hemmons.

CHAPTER FOURTEEN

Riley was reaching for her sword before her eyes were fully open. She swung her legs off the bed and grabbed for a hilt that wasn't there. There was no sheath attached to her side.

A blanket fell to the floor, and Riley realized she was sitting down.

She blinked.

Her sword wasn't on her hip.

She was wearing a light-blue gown, certainly nothing she owned.

The room was empty, and she suddenly felt dizzy. She groaned, leaning forward. She *needed* to lie down but didn't *want* to. She had to understand what was happening around her.

A few moments passed, and the feeling in her head faded slightly. She opened her eyes again and started methodically checking her body with her mind.

Injury, left arm.

She lifted the gown's sleeve and saw a white bandage, so

she peeled it back and looked at the wound. A blade had done it, although Riley couldn't remember when or how. It had been sewn up and was healing. She put the bandage back in place and continued checking herself.

Soreness all over, but nothing broken. Her head hurt, but she was thinking clearly.

WILLIAM!

Her mind shouted the name because Riley had been taking care of him. Riley had dragged him for days and days, and where was he now?

She shot up, ignoring the woozy feeling that washed over her.

"Right Hand, please!" The door in front of her opened and a doctor walked in, already talking. "Please sit down."

"William. Where's William?" Riley didn't stop moving, and even in her poor state, easily sidestepped the doctor when he tried to grab her shoulders.

She continued to the door, pulling it open.

"Right Hand Trident, you need to rest!" the doctor called from behind her, hurrying to catch up now because Riley was already in the hallway.

"Where's William!?"

Riley thought she was in New Perth's castle, but she couldn't be sure. Memories were coming back to her that she didn't fully understand, and yet she couldn't think of anything besides finding William, the other Right Hand.

She turned the corner and stopped in her tracks.

The Prefect stood before her. He was dressed in his usual white robe.

"William is fine."

The doctor rushed into the hallway. "I'm sorry, Your Grace. I'm sorry. I tried to stop her."

"It's okay." The Prefect didn't break eye contact with Riley. "William awoke a day ago. He nearly tore down the castle to find you, and I told those taking care of you that the moment you woke up they were to alert me. I knew you'd do the exact same thing, and I don't want the headache or the expense."

Riley looked down at the floor in reverence of the Prefect. "He's okay, Your Grace?"

"Yes. He's still banged up, but he's going to be fine. He's sleeping now from what I've been told. I've had regular updates on both of you brought to me. It's you and I who need to talk, though. And this isn't a moment too soon."

"Your Grace," the doctor spoke from behind Riley, "she is still not well. She needs more rest."

The Prefect nodded. "I understand, but our city does not care what *we* need. It only cares what *it* needs, and right now, it needs her. Right Hand, I trust that you are still willing to die for the city you've sworn to protect, as well as my son?"

Riley looked up, her eyes bright with intensity. "I am."

"Then come. We have much to discuss."

With that, the Prefect turned and started walking. Riley didn't look back at the doctor as she followed. Her head hurt and her body was sore, but none of that mattered. The Prefect had said she was needed so she would serve.

The two made their way upstairs, Riley noticing that the hallways were oddly empty. She saw no guests, no maids, and no servants. Not even any guards. It was as if only she and the Prefect were in the building.

They went to his quarters, ignoring the court where meetings with him usually occurred. She'd never been to his personal quarters, and she did her best to keep from glancing around as she entered. That wouldn't be proper.

"Please sit, Riley." The Prefect dropped the formal title and sat at a small table next to a window.

Riley stopped and stared out the window.

She'd never seen so much movement.

"What…" she began, completely forgetting who she was with.

"We're preparing for war, Riley, based on what you told us."

Her head snapped back to the Prefect. "What *I* told you?"

Goland nodded. He looked at the table, taking a cigarette paper and some tobacco into his hands. "Yes. You told us that *he* was coming for you, and for New Perth. Do you remember that?"

"No, Your Grace. Not at all."

"Please sit, Riley."

She did, pulling out a chair. "Lucie? Did she make it back?"

The Prefect shook his head. "No. We've seen nothing of her yet."

Riley watched as the old man slowly spread the tobacco along the yellow paper.

"I've started smoking again. Corinth, the doctor, tells me I can't do it for long or the cough will return, and I told him that this coming war can't last long then, or I'll be coughing all damn day."

The Prefect laughed, but Riley remained silent.

"I believe you, Riley. That's not what I want to talk about right now. When William woke up, he said some things that surprised me quite a bit, and I wanted to ask you about them."

Riley looked up, finding the Prefect's eyes on hers.

"If it was anything bad, Your Grace, I can promise you he lied. William *is* a scoundrel, after all."

The old man grinned, understanding the joke. "For once, William spoke highly of you. He told me all about the man in the north. He remembers almost everything quite clearly, and I'm glad of that. If not, I'd probably be smoking twice as many of these, and Corinth downstairs would never stop bothering me. There's magic in the north, and it's coming for us. I feel confident about that. Our scouts tell us no one is coming yet, but that doesn't mean anything."

He finished rolling the cigarette and grabbed a match, striking it and bringing the flame to the cigarette. He breathed in deep, waving the match out with his hand. He placed it on the table, removed the cigarette from his mouth, and let the smoke out.

"I've missed this. I can't deny it." He looked at Riley. "The man's name is Rendal. That's what William said. Do you remember him?"

Riley nodded, a sudden image appearing in her mind. A tall man, strong, almost elegant-looking except for his ruthlessness. His pale-blue eyes were in the forefront of her mind.

"Well, if it's the Rendal I once knew, and I think it is, our scouts might not be able to see anything. He might be shielding them from the naked eye." He took another hit of the cigarette and shook his head. "Perhaps my father was wrong about magic, but there isn't time to dwell on that now. We are where we are, and if he's coming, we have to hope my father wasn't *too* wrong. I'll get to the point, Riley, since time is short. William says that both of you were about to die, and then you *exploded*. I think his turn of phrase was, 'She blew everybody the fuck up, Your Grace.' Always proper, that one."

Riley laughed. "We should charge him every time he curses, sir. We could fund the kingdom for the next hundred years."

"Probably a thousand years, but William would surely starve to death. Every coin he owns would be owed to the castle." He looked directly at Riley. "Did you use magic to save everyone?"

Riley's heart thudded in her chest. She could feel it in her head, which caused the pain to grow worse. "I'm not sure."

"Think. This is important, Riley."

She closed her eyes, more memories coming to her.

They'd been in danger. Everyone. The mage was throwing fire, and it was burning Riley as she rushed forward. William had been to her right, taking a beating that was surely going to end his life. Riley couldn't reach the mage, Rendal, and then—

It'd risen up in her.

She'd felt it before, but nothing like *that*. It was a force like a rising wave, going higher and higher until she could do nothing about it. It filled her very *veins*, an unstoppable force that would either be let loose or destroy her.

She had let it go.

Riley remembered the fire. It rushed from every part of her body, not just her hands. It sprang forward, eagerly reaching out to eat everything around it.

Everything but William.

The fire had spared him…how? Unless it was…

"Magic," she whispered. She opened her eyes and looked at the Prefect. She nodded. "Yes. It had to be."

"Oh, thank the Father and Mother and any other deity who might be listening." The Prefect smiled widely, momentarily forgetting about his cigarette. "I need you to do it again."

"What?"

"Yes. I need you to use your magic when Rendal gets here. New Perth needs you to. I do. Mason does. We all do."

Riley laughed in shock and quickly clamped her mouth shut. What Goland was asking made no sense. "I can't."

"Yes, you can. Just do it again."

Riley laughed, unable to help herself. "Your Grace, I don't know how I did that. I don't have the first clue. I was in danger. *William* was in danger. It just happened."

The Prefect leaned back in his chair, his smile fading. "This isn't good."

"What do you mean?"

As she asked the question, a voice boomed from outside. It spread across the entire city of New Perth and Riley jumped to her feet, reaching for the sword she still didn't have. She stared out the window, a chill growing in her stomach at what she saw.

An army.

Outside New Perth's gates.

"Prefect and good people of New Perth, I bring greetings from my master Rendal Hemmons. He has a demand, and in his graciousness, will spare all of your lives if that demand is met. Prefect Ire, come to your gates and recognize my master's grace."

The Prefect stood much slower than Riley. He turned to the window and then to Riley. "Recognize them?"

"Oh, yeah. The one who's talking is a jackass, and from what I can tell from here, he's brought a lot of other jackasses with him."

"Jackasses are good for tilling soil. Let's go down there and remind them of that, shall we?"

The purple robe was new so it didn't move as easily as the other had, Riley noted. She worried briefly about wearing it in battle, where even a tenth of a second could mean life or death.

She strapped her sheath to her side, then slid her sword in. Riley had inspected the sword the moment it was in front of her, and it looked perfect. Everything else in this world might fall away, including New Perth if the mage had his way, but her sword would survive.

"I didn't think it was possible, but you're even skinnier now."

Riley turned around. William stood in the doorway.

"Looks like you lost some weight too. I might not be able to call you chubby anymore. You think you're still strong enough to fight?"

"Strong enough to kick *your* ass." William came through the doorway but stopped before he reached her. Riley thought he wanted to grab her and hug her, but he didn't. That wasn't his way. Instead, he stuck his hand out. "Thank you. I mean it."

She smiled. "You're going soft, but you're welcome. I'd do it a thousand times, and I mean that too."

The two shook hands, his giant one enveloping hers.

"Let's go see what this fucker downstairs wants," William declared.

"It doesn't look like Rendal came with him." Riley double-checked her bed, making sure she had everything, then turned, following William to the door.

"I doubt he can do much of anything after the burn you gave him. Prefect Ire was mighty happy to hear about it."

The two started down the stairs.

"He wasn't nearly as happy when I told him I couldn't do it again."

"What do you mean, you can't do it again?" William asked as they wound downward.

"Is everyone in this castle... Well, everyone besides Prefect Ire... Well, actually, are *you* an idiot? Do you think I practice magic in my spare time? Sit around conjuring spells or whatever other nonsense those mages do?"

"I don't know whatcha do. You don't practice your sword work enough, I can tell you that, or else we wouldn't have had to use magic. I was fending off about ten men by myself. Just fine, I might add."

Riley caught the slight smirk on his face as he continued, "You couldn't handle one mage until you used magic, so what I'm thinkin' is that you're going to need to figure that shit out if you're to survive this."

Riley could have kicked him down the stairs, but at the same time, she was glad to hear him joking with her.

"You know I saved your ass, William."

He laughed. "Perhaps, but don't tell anybody."

They made their way to the front of the castle where the Prefect was waiting for them. He'd briefly told Riley where Mason was—gone to find mages. Riley's first thought had of course been had been to follow him, but she knew that wouldn't help anyone.

"The army is ready?" Prefect Ire asked.

"Yes, Your Grace," both Right Hands responded.

"Let's go meet the mercenary."

The three mounted their horses, with the Prefect taking the center. As they walked through toward the outer gates, people lined the road, their eyes full of fear. Riley knew nothing like this had ever happened to them before. No army had ever come to New Perth making demands.

This was new.

This was frightening.

And they didn't even know the half of it.

Riley kept her face determined, which was the only thing she could give these people right now. A look that said, "I will win. I will defeat any man who tries to cross our borders."

Archers lined the walls, all of them looking outward. Preliminary counts put the number of men outside the walls at two hundred. It wasn't a large army, but that wasn't the point. A force was here, and more was coming. Might already be coming.

Rendal had cloaked his army from the scouts New Perth had sent. They would have had to literally run into one of the soldiers to know they were there. Another ten thousand could be stationed a mile away, and no one would know.

They reached the tall stone gates, which opened slowly, the machinery creaking in protest as the stone swung. They stood a hundred feet tall, dwarfing even William.

The three walked ten feet beyond the walls, Prefect Ire in front.

Riley wished Mason were here next to his father, yet part of her was glad he wasn't facing this danger.

He has his own danger, she thought. *And I mine, so I have to pay attention to the army in front of me.*

Hundreds of men stood before her, the sun beating down on them all. Riley was sweating, and her head still hurting.

Harold—she remembered his name—stood in front, flanked on either side by men Riley didn't recognize.

Prefect Ire led the way over the bare ground, their horses kicking up dust behind them.

Let those archers be ready, Riley prayed as she approached Harold and his two sidekicks.

"Right Hand Trident, Right Hand Teller, pleasure to see you both again." Harold stopped his horse. Although Riley and William had lost weight, Harold was still hulking. He looked even bigger now, despite the hard four-day trip he'd just made. "Prefect Ire, well met. My name is Harold, and I serve Rendal Hemmons, who I'm sure you're aware was once a citizen of this city."

"I know Rendal." The Prefect spat on the ground. "I also know that if you and your army don't remove yourselves, Rendal and the rest of you will be at war with New Perth.

The archers you see behind me will lay you all out, and the vultures will be picking your bones by nightfall."

Harold chuckled. "As tempting as that sounds, I hope that it doesn't come to war. My master wishes peace, although, like everything, it has a price."

"Peace has no price," the Prefect replied.

Riley and William were quiet. Riley's sword remained in its sheath, although William held his. His knuckles were white.

"*Our* peace does," Harold responded. "It's quite simple. My master wants the woman to your left, Right Hand Trident. He says that if you willingly give her up, he will leave New Perth alone. You will have your peace. He only wishes her to come back with us to our compound."

"*I'll* come back with you!" William shouted, hopping off his horse and forgetting all about etiquette. "I'll come back and cut you all to fucking pieces!"

"Right Hand!" Prefect Ire shouted. "To me!"

William stopped, although Riley could see the effort it took.

Harold smiled down at him. "Go, dog. Your owner calls."

Riley almost spun off her horse at that moment. It was a great honor for the Prefect to command a person in such a way, to trust that he will listen to his words no matter what because his duty to him is that strong. And this man besmirched that honor.

William backed up, although he didn't take his eyes off Harold.

"So, Goland Ire." Harold looked at the Prefect. "What's

it going to be? Give me the woman, and your city can have peace."

"We're done here." Prefect Ire turned his horse and started back toward the gates.

"Hiya, pretty," the man next to Harold commented. "Why don't you come back with us? I'll give you a good time before I give you to the boss."

Riley hadn't truly had time to consider exactly *what* these cretins were asking, but she considered that proposition loud and clear.

"Why don't you come take me right now, and we'll see who has a good time?"

The man looked at Harold, who only shrugged. The man hopped off his horse.

Riley glanced at the Prefect. He'd stopped and was looking at the two of them. "No. We are done here."

Riley turned back to the man on the ground. "Remember me. I'll be the last face you ever see."

She whipped her horse around, and the three marched back into the gates.

***

"They're not leaving," William said.

The three of them were in the Prefect's quarters. His head general, Verith, stood at the edge of the room. People came and went, passing messages to the general, but he'd said nothing so far. Riley knew he would interrupt when he needed to, but for now, he was leaving the discussion to the Right Hands and Ire.

The army had set up camp outside, and fires burned in the darkness beyond the gates.

To Riley, it looked like tiny dots of hell across the landscape.

"They think we're going to give her up," Goland remarked.

"They'll be waiting a long time, then. I'm not very fond of skinny over there, but I sure as hell ain't giving her up to them." William stepped away from the window and walked to the middle of the room, looking as if he wanted to do something, but he didn't know what.

Riley had been silent. The "her" they were talking about was, as everyone knew, Riley, but she hadn't commented. She'd been thinking, though. Almost constantly.

"Why not?" she asked.

"Why not what?" William whirled.

The Prefect looked at her. "Yes. Why not what?"

"Why *not* give me to them? If it keeps New Perth safe, then that's my role. That's what I signed up for—to serve at all costs, including my life. Why not give me up and keep everyone here safe?"

"Father and Mother, she's lost her mind!" William shouted, starting to pace.

"Well, for one, because Mason would castrate me when he returns," the Prefect said. "Although that's beside the point. We're not giving you up, not for peace nor world domination. You took an oath to New Perth, and it also took an oath to you not to betray you. You have stood by your oath, and we will stand by ours."

"Then what do we do, Your Grace? Wait until Rendal gets here and lays waste to the city?"

William stopped walking. "Do you hear yourself? You're mad! You go with them, and they'll do unspeakable things! Unspeakable!"

"Oh, chubby, since when has anything been unspeakable to you?"

"You know what I'm saying!"

Riley turned back to the Prefect. "I'm willing to go, Your Grace. If it helps the city, I'll consider it my honor to go."

"No, and that's the last I'll hear of it. This is actually working in our favor." He looked at Verith. "Tell them."

"They're wasting time by doing this. Had they attacked with magic immediately it would have been a harder fight. Scouts have brought back word that Mason will reach us in two days, and he has strangers with him. If he's brought mages, Rendal's bargain will seem foolish when war comes."

Mason, Riley thought, her heart soaring despite the terror outside the city walls.

He was safe. He'd be here soon. That was what mattered.

"Listen," Prefect Ire said, "I'm growing tired. Verith, there's a constant watch on them, right?"

"Yes, Your Grace. Any movement, and you'll be notified immediately."

"Then I'm going to sleep. I don't think war is coming tonight, and most likely not until Rendal shows up. You two need more rest than I do. Go to sleep, and tomorrow we'll resume planning."

William and Riley left, knowing that the old Prefect

needed to go to bed. They made their way up to their quarters, but William stopped at her door.

"Don't do anything stupid, skinny. You understand me? You may find that man earlier today attractive, but we need you here, not waltzing around with him outside."

"Chubby, do you think you'll lose me to the first man who shows up and says he wants to rape me? Sorry, but you're stuck with me as long as the Prefect says so."

He stared at her for a second longer. Riley wasn't sure if he believed she wasn't going to do something stupid.

"I'll see you in the morning," he told her.

"Not if I see you first."

"Keep it up, and you'll see whatever is beneath your window when I toss you out of it."

"Yeah, yeah. Goodnight, William."

He left Riley alone in her room. She shut the door behind him and sighed, her left hand immediately beginning to shake.

She'd told him and the Prefect that she wasn't going to do anything stupid, and that'd been the first lie she'd ever told either one.

She was *definitely* about to do something stupid.

The most stupid thing she'd ever done, or would ever do.

Riley had tried to get Goland's permission, but he wouldn't give it. So, she was going to defy his wishes. Riley was going outside the city walls and letting those bastards take her wherever they wanted.

If it would give New Perth peace, she had no other choice.

Harold was partially awake, although his chin kept falling to his chest. The fire in front of him burned hot, and that was adding to his sleepiness.

He was waiting on those idiotic New Perthians to hand over the woman. He couldn't actually believe they'd risk war over one person, even one as skilled as she. Granted, there was probably the thought lurking in the back of the Prefect's mind that if he did this once, he'd do it forever. Another group would show up demanding something, and he'd have to give in.

Harold thought it a possibility, but a remote one.

New Perth wasn't going to be attacked by anyone else, and if the Prefect had a lick of sense, he'd understand that.

So Harold waited. He wanted to go back with the Right Hand...and he wanted some time alone with her. Not for anything sexual, but because he wanted to know the truth. Was she more powerful? Should he pledge himself to her?

Harold waited.

It was well past midnight, Harold's head having finally come to rest on his chest when she spoke.

"Hey. Wake up."

Harold's head snapped up, and he found himself staring at the woman. The hood over her head hid most of her face, although the fire's light revealed some features. Her sword was at her side, and she wore all black, including gloves.

She looks like a damned thief, he thought as he struggled to get to his feet. His own sword was on the ground, and he grabbed it on the way up.

She could have slit my throat right there.

Yet she hadn't. The Right Hand stood without moving.

"I'll go with you. Right now. You pack up your army, and we head north. You give me your word that if I do this, Rendal will keep away from New Perth?"

Harold wanted to laugh. His word. There was no *word* here, only the master's rule.

"You have my word."

"Okay. Can Rendal see me right now?"

Harold's eyebrows raised. "Can he? Yes, I'm sure he can. The master's sight has no bounds. The question is, is he looking at you?"

"I don't understand magic, but if he sees me now, can he hear me?"

Harold nodded. "Yes, if he's looking, he can hear too."

"Then he needs to shield us. Or rather, he needs to make it look like you're still here, all these fires are still burning. They're watching up on the walls, and if they see you leave, they'll come looking for me. If your master wants me, he'll have to make sure they think you're still here."

Harold understood what she was saying, but he wasn't too concerned about it. Harold had hitched his horse to the master because the master was powerful and smart. Shielding them was Rendal's business, and he trusted Rendal to handle it.

His was bringing this woman back.

As was making sure no one saw that his loyalty was in question, at least until he knew his next move.

"I'm positive that he'll take care of it."

The Right Hand stared at him for another second and then nodded. "Let's go, then."

"First, tell me why? I can usually smell a trap, but I don't smell anything with you. You came of your own accord. Why?"

"Because I'm not going to let the good people of New Perth die so that I might live. You're a bunch of psychopathic pricks, but I'd rather you have *me* than everyone in there."

Harold shrugged. "I wish I could say I admire your nobility, but I don't. It's moronic. However, this is good news for me. Go ahead and take that sword off, dear."

The Right Hand's eyes widened for a split second, and Harold recognized that look.

Losing her sword was like losing an appendage.

This woman was a true warrior, and he'd do well to remember it. Harold thought if he forgot it for even a second, he might lose his nutsack.

Riley pulled at the belt on her waist, and it started falling. Her hand was lightning quick, grabbing the sword hilt and holding it. The sheath and belt fell to the ground, but the sword remained in her hand, not falling with them.

She tossed it forward gently and with skill, catching the blade but not harming herself. She gave the hilt to Harold, not taking her eyes from his.

"Careful. It's sharp. I wouldn't want it to open your stomach."

Harold smiled. "Me either."

He took the sword.

"Belarus!" he shouted. He'd half-hoped the damned old Prefect would let the woman kill his second-in-command at the gates, but alas. Harold was stuck with the oaf for now.

He heard rustling across the camp and the man stood up, a campfire showing his silhouette.

"Yeah, boss?"

"Get over here!"

The doofus rushed across the camp, kicking and stepping on people as he came. There were grunts and cursing, but Belarus kept on.

"Yeah, boss?" he asked again.

His eyes found the Right Hand.

"Oh, *hell* yes …."

"Close your jaws, Belarus. We've got her, but I need to chain her up. Get the wrist and ankle links. Be quick about it."

Belarus was looking at the young woman as if she were a hunk of roasted meat and he a man who hadn't touched a morsel in days.

"You hear me, Belarus?" Harold's voice grew lower and deadlier. "Get the links."

Belarus nodded, still not taking his eyes from her. "Can I taste her, boss? Just once. Just for a second."

"You'll taste my steel if you stand there ten more seconds. Move."

Belarus blinked, breaking his trance.

Harold watched him go, then turned back to the woman. Her eyes followed Belarus.

"I'm going to kill him." The Right Hand looked at Harold. "And that's bad news for you because if I get loose to kill him, I'm going to kill you too."

"I'm not too worried about it, dear."

Belarus came back carrying the heavy chains. Harold tossed the woman's sword to the ground, noticing with sweet satisfaction the flash of anger that crossed her face.

He held up the wrist links. "From Right Hand to prisoner. The mighty fall and the meek rise. Am I right, Belarus?"

"Right is right, boss. Right is right."

CHAPTER FIFTEEN

William could feel the vein in his head pulsing. Actually *pulsing*, his heart beat with such ferocity.

"It's not fucking possible. It's not fucking *POSSIBLE!*"

His voice spread out over the open expanse, echoing off the walls and gates behind him.

No one was in front of him to hear it. Verith stood behind him, and a host of soldiers behind the general.

The Prefect was still in the castle.

Riley was not.

And the army, the army William had watched until his fucking eyes shut on him last night, was *gone.*

William had woken this morning and known something was wrong. For one, he looked outside, and the damned fires were still burning. The sun was up, so the army wouldn't still have fires going. They would have cleaned that shit up and got to the business of being pains in the collective ass of New Perth.

They were gone.

Riley was gone.

And William knew what *that* meant.

"She fucking lied to me." He turned around and looked at Verith as if it might be *his* fault. "She fucking *lied*, and now she's gone with those psychopaths."

William wanted to attack someone—anyone, and perhaps everyone. All at once.

"We'll send scouts," the general said.

"Scouts? Scouts! The scouts will have better luck seeing each other's dicks than the army. They're shielded, just like they were when they came down here, and just like they were last night. No, they're gone, and the only way we're getting her back is to get up to that compound."

Verith said nothing. His loyalty was to New Perth, and he would do nothing without the Prefect's blessing.

My loyalty is to the Prefect too, William thought.

To hell with that. Goland better send us after her or I'll go alone.

William had never thought something so subversive about the Prefect, but he couldn't help it. They had to get Riley. She'd saved his *life*.

William walked past Verith and went through the troops behind him, the men moving out of his way without thinking. To get in William's path at that moment would not end well for the offender.

William wound his way to the castle and did not pause as he entered the Prefect's quarters.

"She left," Goland told him as he entered. He was staring out his window at the now-empty spot in front of the gates. The false fires disappeared.

William dropped to his knees in front of Goland.

"Please, Your Grace. Please. We must go get her, and if not the army, then send me. I'll go alone."

The Prefect looked down at his Right Hand. "Mason will return tomorrow. We will wait until then."

His voice was soft but firm. He had ruled without challenge for decades, and his voice said that even though his directive might hurt, he expected it to be followed.

"Your Grace, I'm beggin' you."

"Mason will be here tomorrow, hopefully with mages. We will be better able to see what to do then. To go now is foolish, William. You must see that. It will take them four days to return to their compound."

William stood up, just barely able to keep his anger in check.

"They're not going to kill her, my Right Hand."

"You don't know that. He tried to when we were there."

William shook his head.

"I know Rendal. He wasn't trying to kill her. He was testing her."

"Boss, do ya think the boss will let me have a go at her?"

Riley heard the bastard ahead talking about her. He hadn't stopped since they began their retreat.

Have a go.

Get at her.

The phrases didn't matter. They all meant the same thing, and Riley was sick of hearing it. She'd made her choice to go with this group of cretins and she would deal with the consequences, but listening to him talk about it was almost unbearable.

For Harold's part, Riley felt pretty positive he hated his underling. Belarus was just too stupid to see it. The rest of the troops traveled behind Riley; she was between them and Harold. Belarus came and went between the larger group and his boss, seeming not to realize he wasn't wanted.

The rest of the troops had no problem seeing it.

Riley wasn't one to usually provoke people, but this was day one. She had the rest of it plus three more before she'd be rid of this jackass, and she wasn't sure she could take him talking the entire time.

"Hey, Belarus." Riley spoke as the horse moved easily beneath her weight. "Don't you see your boss doesn't want anything to do with you? Look at the rest of your crew. They're behind, where they belong. Why are you even up here to begin with?"

The man whipped around on his horse, bright red embarrassment flooding his cheeks.

"I'm his damned second-in-command. That's why I'm up here. Now shut your fuckin' mouth."

Riley smiled; it was working. Harold had yet to turn around.

"No, you're not up there because you're his second-in-command, you silly jackass. You're up there because you're trying to get permission to rape me. Tell it true—am I wrong?"

Belarus snapped his head to Harold. "I'm gonna make her keep her mouth shut one way or another."

"I'm only a few feet away, Belarus. No need to get

permission from your boss. Just come on back here and break my jaw. I'm sure Rendal won't be too mad about it. Plus you won't have to listen to me yapping the whole way, because I'm not going to stop."

"Boss, ya hear her? She ain't stoppin'. She says she ain't gonna stop."

"I hear her, Belarus. I'm right next to her, as are you." Harold still didn't turn around, but Riley heard the anger in his voice.

"You gonna let me do something?"

Harold sighed, and Riley felt elation. Even bound in chains, she could easily kill this man. While she outmatched him physically and mentally, she'd feel no guilt. She'd be doing the world a favor.

If she wasn't allowed to kill him, injuring him would suffice. It would at least keep him quiet for the next few days.

"What would you like to do, Belarus?" Harold asked.

"Can I break her jaw?"

Harold chuckled, shaking his head. "I could let you try, but I think *you* might come away with the broken jaw."

"You gotta be kiddin' me, boss. I can handle that little girl."

"You couldn't handle me in bed, Belarus, let alone in combat." Riley laughed.

"I'm gonna break her jaw or shove my sock so far down her throat she chokes." His face was turning even redder, a vein pulsing in his neck. He was growing angrier by the second.

Harold sighed again. "Belarus, go on and do what you want to her, but if she hurts you, don't come crying to me."

"HOLD THE LINE!" Belarus shouted, sticking his hand up and stopping his horse. He turned it around so that he was facing Riley full on. "All right, ya little bitch, now you're gonna see what talkin' so much gets ya."

He hopped off his horse, pulling a small mallet from his belt. Riley knew the weapon—in New Perth, they called it a skull-breaker. Good for hand-to-hand combat, especially when your enemy only had their *hands*.

Criminals used them, and they were pulled out when bar fights got vicious, too.

Riley hopped off her horse. She knew this would be slightly more dangerous than usual; her hands were bound with only about a foot in between them. She could still use her legs, but her hands would be a problem.

"Belarus," she remarked as the man started squaring up. "I can see your dick in those pants. If that's what you wanted to rape me with, you might want to use someone else's. That little thing won't get the job done."

Belarus screamed unintelligibly, and Riley focused at that moment. Her jest had gotten her what she wanted, him angry and rushing forward, but now her mind only cared about his movements.

He swung and Riley dodged, the wind from the mallet brushing her face. Belarus wasted no time, swinging a second time in an uppercut fashion.

Riley spun left, only able to dodge the man as he attacked.

Belarus stopped and laughed.

"Is this the girl everyone's so scared of? The one stumblin' 'round in front of me?"

"Belarus, have you hit me yet? This *girl* is avoiding your best shots, and my arms are chained."

Belarus spat and came forward again, moving slower this time. Riley watched, her hands out in front of her.

Belarus swung from the right, the mallet ripping through the air. Riley stepped into the swing, opening her arms and catching his wrist in her chain.

She kept moving around, bending his arm as she twisted hers.

His wrist's snap was audible.

Belarus shrieked, but Riley wasn't done. She was going to kill the bastard if she could. She unwrapped the chain from his wrist and whirled around behind him, dropping it over his neck.

She pulled hard, immediately cutting off his oxygen supply. He started gurgling, spit foaming out of his mouth.

"Now, Belarus, what were you saying? You wanted a go at me?" Riley whispered into his ear.

"Release him."

She felt the tip of the sword in her back. Riley had heard Harold dismount, knowing he was coming to stop the assault. Nothing escaped her senses, but to try to fight him right now would be disastrous.

"Remember, you vicious twit, I'm going to be the last face you ever see. I promise."

Riley raised her hands, letting Belarus go. He fell to the ground, his wrist broken and his neck swelling horribly.

"I told you, Belarus." Harold still held the sword to Riley's back. "You didn't want to hear me, though. Now get your ass back there with the rest of the troops."

Belarus rolled in the dirt, slowly climbing to his feet. He

looked at Riley as he passed her on the way to his horse, and his eyes said what his mouth no longer would. He wanted to kill her.

Come and get it, she thought. *Just come and get it, you fucking prick.*

Night came, and Riley was kept away from the rest of Rendal's army. They'd tied her to a tree, her arms and legs still bound, and given her a quarter ration of gruel. Riley ate it because she knew how important it was to keep her strength up.

She had left with these losers, but she had no intention of missing an opportunity to kill them all.

She wasn't heading to the compound to die or whatever else these fools might have in mind. She was heading to the compound to try to burn it down.

So, if they gave her gruel, she ate gruel.

Riley heard someone approaching from behind her, despite the fact that they were moving extremely carefully. The people keeping her prisoner sincerely had no idea how dangerous she was or how powerful her focus and attention to detail could be. There was no sneaking up on Riley Trident, Right Hand of Mason Ire.

"If you touch me, I can kill you from here." She meant it too. Her torso was tied to the tree, but she could wrap her legs around a man's neck easily, snapping it like a twig.

"I didn't think I could get close to you without you knowing."

It was Harold.

But he hadn't come from the camp in front of Riley. He'd come from behind her, meaning he hadn't been trying to sneak up on *her* but *away* from the camp.

He didn't want any of the soldiers to see him.

Harold kept his distance as he circled behind the tree, both to show her he wasn't here to hurt her, but also to make sure she didn't hurt him.

"What do you want?"

"You're deadly." Harold stopped in front of her.

"You snuck away from your soldiers to tell me something I already know?"

"My boss—"

"Your *master*," Riley interrupted.

"Whatever word you want to use is fine with me. I didn't come out here to debate on that subject. I came to discuss the future."

Reilly's eyes narrowed.

"The future?"

"Yes."

"Whose future?"

"Yours. Mine."

Riley didn't know where this was going, but she thought it would be dumb to ignore it completely. "What are you getting at?"

"My boss is going to want you to join him. To serve him as I do."

"Well, his ass is going to be sorry if that's the case. I'm not joining him."

"I thought that might be the case. If you don't join him, it's going to be worse for you."

"Then it'll be worse for me," Riley answered. "I don't care. I don't join psychopaths. I serve New Perth."

"You don't desire to rule?"

"No. Rulers are born to it. I was made a warrior. I want to serve my rulers, and that's it. Now, why the hell are we having this conversation?" Riley was tired of talking to him. She had thought it would be smart to listen, but she didn't have any desire to discuss her philosophy with this man.

"I wanted to hear what you'd say. That was all."

"Well, now you've heard it. I'm not joining your *master*. I'm not joining any part of this organization. I'll die first."

"You may get your wish." Harold looked at her for another second and then walked off, heading back the way he'd come.

Riley listened to his footsteps fade, wondering what the hell the man was planning.

CHAPTER SIXTEEN

"She left?" Mason asked.

"Of her own volition, son."

Mason was stunned. He sat in his father's quarters, William across the room looking out the window at the courtyard below. Worth and the crew he had brought were down there; Mason had had the servants bring them food and drink.

"Spirits, sir?" one servant had asked.

Mason had said yes, but from the sound of things downstairs, that might have been a mistake. The group was growing louder and louder, and from William's cross face —he wasn't pleased.

But now Mason was dealing with the fact that his Right Hand was gone.

"When?" he asked. "When did she leave?"

"Two days ago."

"And you haven't sent anyone after her?"

"No." His father looked at him, his eyes level, but clearly, he didn't like the tone in Mason's voice.

"Why not?" Mason didn't care about the tone. Riley was gone, and the castle sat here as if nothing had changed.

"You're not thinking clearly, Mason." The Prefect looked at William, but the big man gave no sign he was listening. Mason thought that was an act, but he didn't care what William heard. This was ludicrous. "Had I sent someone the moment they left, we probably would not have seen anyone. Rendal holds sway over our minds when we look at them, son. It's a magic I don't understand. We needed magic to battle magic, so I waited for you. Our scouts said you were returning, and you have. Now we can discuss our alternatives."

The Prefect turned again to William and the window.

"I don't think those people out there are from Sidnie. Am I correct?"

"Yes," Mason answered. In the desert at the tent city, he hadn't thought through what his father might think of this choice. It'd simply been one of survival more than anything else.

Now, he realized he was being judged.

For the way they looked.

He could almost see it in William's face. *Mutants.*

"May I ask why you didn't continue to Sidnie as you were instructed?"

"And if I had, Father, where would we be now? I'd be another eight days away, at least, and Riley would most likely be dead."

The Prefect said nothing for a second, then stood up and walked across the floor to the window.

"They're a lively bunch."

William snorted but said nothing.

"The question is, do they know magic, son? And can they follow orders? If we're going to war, then they must be able to help. If not, there's no point in heading north. We should simply try to fortify our defenses here."

Mason stood. "Come on, let's go see what they can do."

William followed the two Prefects downstairs toward the courtyard, where the group of mutants was getting drunk. Personally, William thought Mason had lost his damn mind. He'd been sent to Sidnie for mages, and he'd brought back *mutants*.

They made William's skin crawl. He'd never met any before, but he'd heard about them. He wondered if it might be contagious; if perhaps one of the extra appendages growing off their arms or legs might somehow spread to him. He'd wake up with a finger sticking out of his forehead or something.

Mason had lost his mind, that was for sure.

The other sure thing was that they were wasting time.

They needed to be going to get Riley.

William said none of this, however. It wasn't his place. He served Goland and Mason would one day take his father's place, even if he was now batshit crazy.

They entered the courtyard and William nearly groaned.

The place was a mess.

They'd been here two hours tops, and three of the strangers were already passed out on the ground. One woman lay on her stomach, her pants halfway off so that her tan ass was staring at everyone.

The leader—his name was Worth and nothing else from what William gathered—sat at a table. A large jug of wine was in front of him, and his lips were purple from drinking it.

He looked at the three men and smiled.

"Strong! Strong drink!"

He laughed heartily.

The Prefect looked mortified, and Mason looked somewhat frightened. None of them had expected this.

A mutant without an arm walked up and draped the one he did have over Worth. He kissed the big man's cheek. "Good. Good food."

He stumbled off merrily back to the other side of the courtyard, where it looked like some kind of card game was being played.

"Have they ever drunk alcohol before?" William asked.

"I don't know." Mason stepped over to the leader. To William, the man didn't appear to have any mutations, but who knew for certain? "Have you had alcohol before?"

"Yes! Yes! Just not in while. Long while. It's gooooood." The man smiled broadly, showing how pleased he was with it.

William's right hand began trembling with rage. The man in front of him was big, but William was about ten seconds away from snapping his neck and throwing the rest of these mutants into the jails beneath the castle.

"Son," Goland started. "This is... What is happening right now?"

Mason said nothing, only stared at Worth.

"Oh, oh. I see. I see." The mutants' leader stood. "This father? He not like drunk?" The big man smiled and swayed a bit. "Sorry. Sorry. I am Worth. You father?"

The Prefect remained quiet, and William thought his other hand might start trembling too. This was an embarrassment to all involved.

"He no like us?" Worth turned to Mason. "Mutants not liked here either?"

Mason shook his head. "No. You're welcome here. You're welcome anywhere I am. My father is the ruler here. Our Prefect. I told him you were magic, and I told him you would help us. The woman, she's been taken—"

"Took?" The drunk man's face showed complete confusion. "Gone?"

"Yes, gone. The mage took her back to his home. We have to go get her, and my father wants to know that you are magic."

William hardly understood the drunk's words, nor did he understand why Mason kept saying things like "you are magic." It was as if he was using their primitive speech.

Insane, all of it, he thought. *The Prefect has to see it and kick these people out. We have to leave. Gather the army and leave.*

"He want magic? If we show magic, he happy?" Worth asked.

"Yes. He'll be happy."

"Ha!" Worth turned around. "Torney!"

William didn't know who he was shouting to but no one looked over.

"Torney!"

Finally, the woman on the ground rolled over. She pulled her pants up, sat up and looked at Worth. "What?"

"They want see magic. Don't believe."

The woman's lips were as purple as Worth's, and when she smiled, her teeth were too. "What see?"

"Your Grace," William whispered, "this is ridiculous. We need to get out of here now. These damn people are no more mages than my ass."

William was still talking when he started to rise into the air. Words flowed out of his mouth as his eyes grew wider.

"What? What is this!" he shouted.

Higher he rose, and he watched as his shoelaces started untying themselves.

Everyone beneath stared up at him, and the mutants were laughing. Hooting, hollering, and pointing as if he was some kind of freaking show.

"PUT ME DOWN!" William bellowed, rage filling his body. He swung his arms left and right and kicked his feet, trying to find some way to get down.

He stopped rising, but his shoes flew from his feet.

"Magic, aye!" Worth shouted from below, slapping his knee. "Magic, his ass!"

William understood then.

"No! No! No!"

It was too late.

His belt was coming undone, and the buttons on his pants were doing the same.

"NO!"

His pants snapped off just as his shoes had.

His underwear came next, and William was naked from the waist down in front of everyone. The laughter from below drowned out everything. Worth was crying now—slapping his knees and actually crying.

William shut up, knowing there was nothing he could do as he was turned over in the air, his bare ass visible to everyone.

Worth spoke from beneath him. "We magic. Tell father we magic and we ready to find woman. We magic, so let's go!"

Mason could barely stop smiling. It was one of the funniest things he'd ever seen in his life, despite the terror of Riley's absence. Goodness, it had been rich.

William didn't think so, of course.

When Torney finally put him down, William tried to kill her. He'd charged across the courtyard like a madman, but that hadn't lasted long. Torney froze him again, and everyone could see William straining, but he hadn't been able to move regardless of what he did.

Everyone kept laughing, including Mason, and that only made William madder.

Finally, things had settled down.

The tent people were sleeping off their drunk, except for Worth, whom Goland had invited back to his quarters.

Now, the three of them sat at a large table—Mason, his father, and Worth. William stood away from the gathering, as was expected of a Right Hand.

He was still fuming, but Mason thought he understood these people's value now. If William tried to kill them, he'd be trying to kill Riley. New Perth *needed* these tent people.

"When do we leave?" Mason asked.

"Hold your horses, son. Worth, how much magic can you do? That was an impressive showing down there—" The Prefect started chuckling, unable to help himself. Mason saw William gripping his hands into fists, but the Right Hand said nothing. "But what else? Taking pants off in midair isn't going to help us defeat Rendal."

Worth nodded. "Yes. Yes. All magic. We do all magic. Have to. Hard world in desert. Must have defense."

"I'm not an expert on magic, Worth," Goland continued. "I know the gist, but not all of it. You can do magic that messes with people's heads, is that correct?"

"Head magic?" Worth asked.

Goland looked at Mason, who shrugged. He didn't know how to answer.

"Yes. You can read minds?"

"Ah!" Worth smiled and showed off his still purple teeth. "Think number."

"Huh?" Goland asked.

"He wants you to think of a number, Father."

"Okaaaay," Goland said.

"Nine. Another."

Goland's eyes narrowed.

"Forty-two. Big man behind wonder how much I weigh. William. Want to throw me through window." He smiled as he spoke, no anger in his eyes. He kept looking at Goland.

The Prefect turned to William. His face was bright red, almost a constant now. "Is that true, William? Were you wondering his weight?"

William nodded.

"We magic. All kind magic," Worth said as Goland turned back to the table.

"I don't know enough about any of this to understand if the man has what it takes." Goland looked at Mason. "I guess we don't have a choice, though. You were right to bring them back, but I have to ask myself, is getting Riley worth it? Is she worth going to war?"

Mason closed his eyes, and when he did, he saw Riley's face. Not when she was in the castle's ward, but when they were younger. He saw her at Lucie's restaurant eating some stew Lucie had given her. Riley's face had been dirty, and when she'd looked up at him, she'd laughed.

You're taller in the parades, was what she'd said, recognizing him immediately.

Mason opened his eyes. "She is."

He saw William's hands relax from the corner of his eye.

"She's worth it, without a doubt."

"How many soldiers do I send?" Goland pulled a pouch of tobacco from his pocket, as well as cigarette papers. "I've never attacked anyone, and neither did my father. This is new. There are so many variables that go into it."

"Your Grace," William commented from behind him, "we might not need to send an army. We have the magical *mutants*. You could send me, Verith, and them. We could be a smaller group, and if those mutants are right, we'll be able to rescue her. We'll move quicker, too."

"And me." Mason found William's eyes. "I'm going too."

His father looked at him. "Heir to the throne, you'd wish to set aside your duty to this city for her?"

"Her duty is to me. Mine is to her."

Goland nodded. "Perhaps."

"Your Grace, we've got to act now," William demanded. "We haven't got time to waste. They have a two-day head start. If we leave right now, she'll have been in that compound for a full two days. That's too long."

The Prefect turned to William. "I know my business, Right Hand."

He sighed, standing up and walking toward the window. He looked down at the courtyard, where the servants were cleaning.

"Or maybe I *don't* know my business. I'm old, and I feel older with each minute that passes. This Rendal man—he's something from the past, and the world forgot about him. He didn't forget about the world, though. I'm sorry, William. You deserve better than for me to snap at you. Your friend is in danger. My son's Right Hand." He nodded, although Mason thought he was nodding to himself rather than to anyone else in the room. He didn't look at them when he spoke next. "Get the tent people, Mason. Go and bring her back. I care more about that than war. Kill Rendal if you can, but your first duty is to bring back the Right Hand. If Rendal wants war after that, we'll prepare."

"You don't have to worry about that, Your Grace," William declared. "If I see that fucking mage, I'll rip his throat out for what he's done."

"We ready go?" Worth stood up, swaying slightly, purple lips smiling. "Go get your woman, aye?"

"Aye," Mason agreed. "Let's go get her."

CHAPTER SEVENTEEN

R endal stood next to Artino.

The man was silent, staring at the person in front of him. He wasn't bustling around the laboratory as usual. He wasn't talking about interruptions incessantly. He wasn't looking at his feet. It happened very rarely, but Artino was in his element.

And Rendal knew what *that* meant.

He thought the experiment would be a success.

And right on time, too. Rendal had been following Harold's progress since he left, and the army would be arriving in an hour or so.

"Is he ready?" Rendal asked, looking at the man across the laboratory. He wore a red necklace. It wasn't lit, but looked dull beneath the bright lights above.

"It's not him that matters, Rendal. It's the equipment."

"Well, Artino, is the *necklace* ready?"

"Equipment, Rendal! Equipment. It's not a *necklace.*" Artino shook his head, then looked at his subject again. "Yes. It's ready. Here."

He handed Rendal a red bracelet.

"I changed the color of it because if you confuse it with your other one, you'll be dead in the water."

Rendal thought he saw a small grin trying to form at the corner of the man's mouth; his own joke on Rendal, perhaps getting him back for all the interruptions. This was his way of calling Rendal dumb.

Rendal didn't give a damn. He took the bracelet and slapped it on his right wrist.

Nothing happened.

"What am I supposed to do, *Artino*?" The damn contraption wasn't working.

"Give it a second. They take time to see each other. You will feel it soon."

Rendal was quiet, looking at the man on the other side of the room. His eyes were open, and he was staring straight into space as if he couldn't see anything.

And then Rendal felt it.

The bracelet on his wrist turned dark red, like the color of blood.

The red necklace across the room lit up too.

"Oh, this is good, Artino. This is very, very good."

"Sir, the woman is in her room."

Rendal could not remember the last time he had been in such high spirits. If he were honest, he hadn't thought Artino's engineering would work. Not this time. What Rendal had asked him to do was too difficult. Nay, Rendal had thought it impossible.

But it *did* work.

Artino was a genius, and when Rendal was Prefect of New Perth, the man would come right along with him.

Harold was here now, and the Right Hand had been returned.

The two stood on the north side of the compound, Rendal having been watching the sea crash against the cliffs below. He felt so good that for once he hadn't been working. He just wanted to watch the sea and enjoy how close he was to his goals finally coming to fruition.

Rendal turned to his head guard.

"How were your travels?"

"They were fine, especially with the cover you gave us."

Rendal smiled. "Times are good, Harold. Times are very, very good, and I have a feeling they're going to get better. Come walk with me for a minute."

Harold stepped forward, and he and Rendal started walking west. The sound of water breaking on the cliffs below made its way to their ears, and the smell of salt was heavy in the air.

"What do you think of her?" Rendal asked.

"She's a devastating fighter," Harold answered.

"Do you think she will bend to my will? Do you think she'll join our cause?"

"No." Harold's eyes narrowed. "I think she'll die first."

Rendal nodded, his feet moving slowly over the bare ground. "They all say that at first, don't they? That they won't join. It's rare, though, that someone doesn't join. Let me ask you, Harold, would you *want* her to join?"

"My opinion doesn't matter, sir. I serve at your leisure."

"I know. I know. But I'm asking your opinion, so humor me. Would *you* want her to join?"

Rendal wanted to see how truthful Harold would be right now. He understood the imbalance Harold was feeling. The man's soul followed power and nothing else. Rendal was the most powerful person he'd ever met, so Harold had fallen right into place.

But if he thought this woman was more powerful, then Harold would follow her. He would switch allegiance because that was how people like Harold survived. You didn't fight power. You joined it.

"If she can serve, then yes, I think she should join. If she cannot serve, then she has no place here. Like I said, sir, she's a devastating warrior. Perhaps the best I've ever seen. She would be a great addition if she will kneel before you."

Rendal was quiet for a few moments. He was looking through Harold's mind, trying to understand if the man was lying.

He couldn't tell, and that was an odd thing. Harold was not complicated. Smart? Yes. Ruthless? Double yes. But complicated? No. The world was black and white to Harold, but right now he seemed to be confused.

And only one thing could have led to that.

Harold didn't know who was more powerful, Rendal or the Right Hand. Rendal or Riley.

Thus, he wasn't sure what to do.

That was fine with Rendal. People like Harold weren't meant to lead. They were followers through and through.

Harold would either recognize Rendal's power, or he would die. It was that simple.

"You did a good job bringing her back," the mage told him. "Now, I think it's time I go see our guest."

They shoved a green necklace onto Riley and threw her in a room.

She heard the door lock as the underlings left. Harold hadn't been near her since they'd arrived at the compound. Rather, he'd let those beneath him handle the work of getting her situated.

No one had spoken to her.

Indeed, outside of Harold and the now-injured Belarus, hardly anyone looked at her.

Riley didn't know what the green necklace had to do with anything. *She* certainly didn't feel anything from it. She wasn't dead, and that was a good thing. She hadn't been harmed in any way, and the pain she had felt days before was almost completely gone.

If she had a chance to fight now, she'd be able to wreck some people.

That was what Riley wanted: a chance to fight, to rip this place apart.

When she heard the knock on the door, her body was already moving, her hand reaching to where her sword should be—but wasn't.

The door slowly opened, and the tall mage stood in its place.

"Hello, Riley."

Riley's eyes narrowed, and her heart hardened with

hate—truly a thing she had not known until this man. "Where is Lucie?"

"She's here." Rendal stepped in a bit farther. "Unharmed, of course."

"You say it like I'm supposed to believe you. You nearly killed the other Right Hand and me. Your words are meaningless. You're scum."

"Oh, Riley, you wound me," Rendal replied. "Lucie is fine. I've had to put a necklace on her like you're now wearing, but other than that, she's perfectly okay. I think you have the wrong idea about me, and I hope I can change that over the next few days."

"Like I'm your fucking guest or something?" Riley wanted to rip his throat out. "You threatened war with my city if they didn't give me up, so I came willingly. You should remember that I'm only here because I decided to be. I could have killed that whole army by myself, and if you doubt me, give me another shot right now."

"No, no." Rendal smiled. "I don't doubt your skill with a sword. And yes, I know you came of your own accord. It was very noble of you. It saved a lot of lives."

Riley gritted her teeth, her jaw flexing. "Let Lucie go."

"Okay, I can do that," Rendal answered. "I'm willing to give up a lot for you, Riley. You'll come to see that soon."

"For me? You'll never have me. I'll sleep with that fool Belarus before I give myself to *you*."

The mage laughed loudly, looking at the ceiling.

"Oh goodness, Riley, that *is* funny. Belarus certainly is a fool, and I saw you snap his wrist. That brought me a lot of happiness, I must say. However, I don't want you like he did. You're going to be an important part of my kingdom. Not a queen, but an heir. You understand?"

"I understand that if you try anything like Belarus wanted, you'll end up with a nub for a dick. And as for being your heir?" Riley smiled. "I think I'll prefer burning this place to the ground."

"Yes, yes. Another reason I think you have finally found your destiny. Loyalty. Nobility. You possess all the necessary traits in an heir. But there will be time to talk about that later. Come, let's eat. We've prepared a feast."

Riley's first instinct was to tell him to fuck himself again, but she had to be smart about this. Going on a hunger strike would do nothing except weaken her body. She needed strength, because there would be a moment when the defenses of this place fell—if even for a second—and she had to be ready.

"Yes?" Rendal asked.

Riley nodded.

"Come, then."

The two walked through the hallways, Rendal leading her to a different dining area than last time.

The food was plentiful, and the smells were mouth-watering. Riley hated herself for it, but she couldn't help feeling ravenous.

"Go on," he instructed. "I can tell you're hungry. Eat. Drink."

Riley glanced at him and, feeling traitorous to New Perth, she went to one of two plates at the table. She piled it high and then sat down, ignoring Rendal completely.

"Why do you think of Mason so much?" Rendal asked.

Riley looked up, and her eyes narrowed. He couldn't know Mason from when he had been in New Perth since her leader hadn't been born yet. Yet he was asking about him?

"He's constantly in your mind," Rendal said as if answering her question. "Even when concentrating on nourishment, you think of him. Why?"

"Don't talk about Mason. Don't even let his name slip from your mouth or I'll kill you with the plate in front of me."

"I have no doubt you'd try. Would you die for him?"

Riley ignored that, focusing on the most important question. "How do you know what I'm thinking?"

The mage moved to the other plate. He was quiet as he put his food on it, though not nearly as much as Riley had taken. He finally sat down across from her.

"You don't understand the power of magic. There are many different kinds, and that's only one of them. I have the ability to wander through people's minds like you might walk through a hallway."

"You can read thoughts?"

Rendal nodded. "Yes."

And I can talk to you through them, too.

Riley stood up, again reaching for a sword that wasn't there. It was *his* voice inside her head.

"Don't do that."

"I'm sorry." He smiled and took a small bite of meat. "It can be a bit shocking at first, I understand. I only wanted to show you what I meant. Please, sit and eat."

Riley paused a second longer, hating him even worse. *He* had been inside her mind, *his* voice filling it.

Like Lucie did when she told you to run.

"Please. I won't do it again," the mage promised.

Riley slowly took her seat again.

"What you did outside with the fire was a basic maneuver, much like the first stance you learned as a fighter. There is so much more to magic than fire." He looked up from his plate, meeting her eyes. "Riley, I've been all across this continent. From New Perth to Sidnie, and even north to the Fallen City. I've been through the Badlands countless times. I've never seen anyone with the magic potential you have. It's greater than mine was at your age. It's greater than all the mages in Sidnie."

Riley looked at the plate in front of her and took a bite of food.

She didn't like hearing this.

She didn't want magic. It wasn't part of her community or her culture.

"But it's a part of you, Riley."

"Get out of my *mind*," she snapped.

Rendal nodded, looking sincere. "Yes. I'm sorry."

She didn't believe him, of course. This was all lies. He'd nearly killed William and her, and now was treating her like royalty. All of it was bullshit.

"With your potential and my knowledge, we could do so much good for people. There are so many things that can help New Perth if only the people would embrace their magic. You and I, we can show them that, Riley. Not through force. Not through war. Simply by living it. You have only to embrace your magic and join me."

Riley looked up, a smile on her face. "Did you think it would be that easy, Rendal? I'd show up, you'd wine and dine me like a cheap date, and then I'd simply join you?"

Rendal shook his head. "No. You wouldn't be the right person if that were the case. We've got time. You'll come to see the truth, that magic is the way of the future, and that you and I can change the whole continent for the better."

Riley thought about keeping her mouth shut, but realized it wouldn't matter. He could just read her mind.

"If we're talking time, you better make sure you keep me away from any weapons. Because the first *time* I see one, I'm going to stick it so deep in your guts you'll wish you'd killed me the first *time* you saw me."

Riley took a bite of her food.

CHAPTER EIGHTEEN

The first day of travel was done, and although William wanted to continue, Mason said no. The crew would be no help to Riley if they showed up without any sleep.

"You. Come. Me make you magic." That was what the bald man told William once they'd all eaten, right before walking away from the camp, leaving the fires behind and venturing into the dark wilderness.

William almost threw an axe at him, but instead, he'd looked at Mason and Verith.

Verith only shook his head, smiling.

"Go on," Mason told him. "Go learn some magic, William. Unless you want what happened to you yesterday to happen again?"

William almost threw the axe at the Assistant Prefect.

Instead, he mumbled, "We don't practice magic."

"Times are changing, Right Hand. Magic might be the only thing that saves us."

"Come! Come!" Worth hollered from the darkness. "I make you magic!"

William shook his head and stood up. He grabbed his broadsword and slapped it across his back. He wasn't sure what was about to happen, but he thought he might have to kill that jolly giant. He was okay with that.

He walked into the darkness and stood in front of Worth.

"Sword. Good." Worth put his hand out in front of him. "Me see. Please."

"You're out of your damn mind. You're not touching my sword."

The smile on Worth's face dropped, and William saw a seriousness there that he understood. A *sincerity*.

It's the same look I see in those I train for battle, the ones who care. The ones who want to serve. Who want to do well. It's the look I take on before battle. It was the look Riley wore, too.

Riley wears, his mind corrected. *She's still alive.*

He took his sword from the sheath and handed it over hilt-first.

"Thank you." Worth squatted, letting the sword lie in both hands. "This like magic. This similar. When you fight, what you feel?"

William shook his head. This was stupid. What did he *feel?*

"Nothing. I kill. That's all."

"Lies, Right Hand. Lies. Think. Don't be dumb. Think. When you fight, what you feel?"

Worth didn't look up but stared at the sword shining in the moonlight. He was serious. He wanted to know what William felt when he went to battle.

The Right Hand closed his eyes.

"The sword is part of me. It's not separate. It's the same

as my hand, something that listens to my commands and immediately does what I want. I imagine it's even more like that for Riley because she's better with it. I feel like my arm has grown an extra four feet."

"Yes. That right. Your arm grows. It is part of you. That like magic. It is part of you." Worth looked up at him. "I show you how magic help? May I?"

William's eyes narrowed. He knew what the man was asking, although not exactly what he meant. "Go on, Worth, but be careful. If you do something dangerous, I'm going to kick your damn teeth in."

"Shh, Right Hand. Shh. I be careful. You watch."

Worth looked down at the sword, and his hand lit on fire. William jumped back, but Worth didn't move. He simply stared at the sword.

And the fire started to spread across the blade.

"Hey!" William shouted, forgetting his fear and moving to protect his blade.

"Shh, shh. The fire is like arm. It part me. It won't hurt sword, also part me. Your hand not hit your face. Same here."

William watched as his silver blade turned into a fiery one.

Worth looked up. "You ready?" He was smiling, a devilish-looking thing that said much more than his words.

William was quiet, having no idea what was about to happen.

Worth stood. "I go there. You stay. You watch." He turned and walked into the night, saying nothing else. William stared after him, his sword a red light in the darkness, flames dancing across it but not blackening it.

The man stopped twenty feet away.

He gripped the sword with both hands, took a step back, and then swiped—a heavy, harsh throw of his arms that looked like a solid swing.

Fire ripped forward, crossing the night air. It moved fast; William might have been able to duck if he hadn't been frozen in awe.

The flame stopped mere inches from his face. William could feel the heat, almost close enough to singe him. He stared, not comprehending what he was seeing. The fire stretched all the way back to Worth, attached to the sword and his hand.

Worth pulled the sword to him and the fire disappeared, remaining only on the blade.

William didn't move as Worth started to swirl the sword. He did it quickly, clearly someone who had been trained in the art of battle. The fire moved with the blade, shooting into the air at times, pulling back at others, and William finally saw what it meant.

What magic could do for someone like him.

On the battlefield protecting his Prefect, he would be a hundred times deadlier if he wielded a blade of fire that stretched as far as he wanted.

Worth stopped slicing with the sword, and the fire died.

He walked back across the expanse and handed the sword hilt-first to William. He was smiling. "I make you magic, aye?"

William took the sword, half expecting it to burn his hand. It didn't. It was the same temperature as when he'd handed it over in the first place.

"Aye. Make me magic."

The two stayed up late, the rest of their crew going to sleep.

"You tired?" Worth asked.

William shook his head. "No. I want to learn this."

"It take time. Long time, sometime."

"We don't have a long time. We have three more days, and if I have to stay up every night learning this, then that's what I'll do."

Worth nodded. "I like. I like."

William was finding it beyond difficult to do anything Worth told him. Anything at all. They'd been at it for hours, and the most William had felt was a slight warmth in his hand, but that might have just been blood flowing from his own frustration. They had a few more hours before the sun came up, and then he'd have to start riding north again.

William wasn't concerned about sleep. He'd been up countless nights in this life, and most of the time it was for what would come in four days: battle.

What he cared about was the fact he couldn't *learn* this.

"Sit. Sit," Worth insisted.

William hated the man bossing him around. No one spoke to him like that, and only the Prefect and his son commanded him, yet he couldn't say anything. If he wanted to learn, he had to listen to this goofy tent dweller.

William sat down on the ground. They'd been at this for hours. William had tried starting with the sword, but the damned tent dweller had only laughed at him. When

William tried to slice through the air and throw fire, Worth fell on the ground holding his stomach.

"You're too fucking fat to be rolling around," William had said.

Now, Worth sat down in front of him. He scooted up close, crossing his legs in front of him so that his knees pointed outward on either side. "Like this."

"You want me to sit like you now?"

"Yes. Like this."

William did it, crossing his legs over one another, though it was hard for him to pull his feet in tightly.

"Tight. Tight," Worth urged.

William glared at him, but the big man only smiled back.

The Right Hand did as he was told, pulling his feet closer to his groin. Worth scooted a little closer, so their knees were touching.

"There. Good. Now, hand. Me see."

Worth put one hand out, palm up. William gave him his left hand.

"Other too."

William extended it, both hands now palm up in Worth's.

"Eyes. Close."

You're doing this for Riley, he reminded himself and closed his eyes.

"Good. Good."

He felt Worth folding one of his hands over the other and clasping them in his large ones.

"Magic inside. It in here." Worth pressed down on his hands. "But not just here. It here, too."

Worth touched the side of his head, and William flinched but didn't open his eyes.

"Most important, here."

He touched the left side of William's chest.

"No might bring magic. Heart bring magic. Why you here?"

William opened his eyes.

"Close!" Worth hissed. When his eyes were closed again, Worth asked again, "Why you here? For who?"

Riley's face came to him. It filled his whole mind.

"Yes. Her. Good. Focus. Find her. Why you here? Her. Find her."

The words Worth spoke at that moment didn't matter, only Riley did. Because she'd saved him, dragged him across hell to make sure he lived, and now he would go through anyone and anything to get her back.

"Good. Good. Keep going. Focus. See her."

He would get her back. He and Mason and this ragtag group of mutants would march into that fucking bastard's compound and burn the whole thing down, and no one was going to stop him. If they tried, he would stomp them into the ground until there was nothing left and—

"Look," Worth told him.

William opened his eyes.

Worth no longer held his hands. They were in front of him, and they were on fire.

"You magic now. You bad student, but you magic."

Mason had seen William's hands light up last night. He'd nearly jumped up from his mat when it had happened.

The man's dedication had been remarkable. Mason watched the entire night. He hadn't moved, though, when the Right Hand finally blazed. He'd remained on his mat, far away so that the two couldn't see he was awake.

He'd let William have the moment because he deserved it. Also, any recognition might have ended it, because William didn't want to practice magic of any kind. Mason knew why he was doing it, and it was the same reason Mason had crossed the Badlands: Riley.

William might not *want* to practice magic, but Mason wanted him to learn. The more people who could light their hands and swords on fire, the better.

William was at the front of the line, his horse leading the way. Verith was behind Mason and Worth directly in front of him.

Mason spurred his horse and trotted up to the tent city leader.

"Aye, Mason." The man didn't turn to look at him, and he wasn't smiling either. The tent city leader was usually smiling almost stupidly. Mason had only seen him look this serious when he had first shown up at the tent city.

"I wanted to talk to you about last night with William."

Worth nodded. "Talk."

"Thank you for doing that. Can you continue? Will you teach him more?"

"He have potential. I make him magic." Worth nodded, still looking forward.

"He's going to need sleep, but teach him as much as you can before we get there, okay?"

"He no need sleep. He warrior. Like Worth. Sleep for babies, not warriors."

Still no smile from the big man, and Mason didn't like that.

"Is something bothering you, Worth?"

He nodded. "Aye."

"What?"

"He watch us."

"Who?" Mason looked around the open landscape. He saw no one, just dead grass and dirt.

"Mage. He see us now. Know we come."

Mason understood, and he looked up as if he would be able to see Rendal Hemmons.

"No. Not up there. All around. He see you. He see me. He dangerous. Powerful."

Mason brought his head back down. "We are too. You and your ilk, plus the Right Hand and Verith. We're powerful, too."

"Worth know. We magic. We be okay."

Mason rode with him for a few more seconds, but it seemed clear that Worth wasn't looking to talk to anyone, so Mason dropped back into line.

He sees us, Mason thought and smiled.

He raised his hand and closed all the fingers but one.

"Get fucked."

Lucie lay against the back of her cage.

Her body looked drained, almost sickly. She was coming to look like the other women in this place.

She looked down as her cage was lowered from the ceiling. Rendal already stood below it. He hadn't come back to her since the first time, and Lucie had been fine with that. She didn't want to see this hollowed-out human anymore. He wasn't the person she had loved.

The cage stopped, but Lucie didn't attempt to get up. She was too weak. She received food and water, but lack of nutrients wasn't causing her to feel like this.

It was the draining, as she was coming to think of it.

"I can tell that you understand what I've become now," Rendal started.

Lucie blinked slowly, showing no emotion on her face. "I can tell you're a madman."

"I have her, Lucie. I have the Right Hand. She's here."

Lucie swallowed. "Have you hurt her?"

"No, of course not. I'm going to make her my protégé. And if not, I'll throw her in this cage with you so that you have company. I'm not completely cruel. In fact, I'd say I'm not cruel at all. I just believe in purpose."

Lucie looked up at the cages above her. "That's not cruel, Rendal?"

"That's purpose." He smiled, though it died away quickly. "Her precious Mason is coming for her, Lucie, and he looks to have mutants with him. Who are they?"

"Mutants?" Lucie's eyebrows raised. She knew nothing about any mutants. There were none in New Perth. Hadn't ever been as far as she knew.

"Yes. I think they're mages. Who are they, and are they are from New Perth?"

"I don't know them, Rendal. And I don't know where they're from, either."

Rendal stared at her, measuring the truth in her words.

"I don't give a damn if you believe me. To be honest, I'd rather stare at the bars on this cage than your face. You're not very handsome anymore, ya know? Why not just raise me back up in the air and let me stare at the bars a while longer?"

Rendal shook his head. "Handsome or not, we're not done here. I don't know who these mages are, but if they practice magic, they could be a threat—mutants or not. I'm going to get you out of there, actually."

"Why?"

"An insurance policy of sorts."

"I can't help you, Rendal. Don't you see that? I'm nothing in New Perth. They've forgotten my part in your failed attempt for power. They don't care about me. If people are coming, then they're coming for Riley—not me. They won't care what you threaten me with."

"You still don't see." Rendal smiled. "All this time, and you still can't see the end. You don't matter to them, Lucie, but you matter to *her*. You matter to Riley, and she's not going to leave as long as you're here. She'll stay out of this little skirmish if she knows you might be injured...or killed."

Rendal stepped back.

"Guards, get her out of there. She's to be our guest of honor for this next battle. And Lucie, don't think I won't kill you if you do something antithetical to my purpose."

Rendal had one other thing to check, then he wanted to

watch the travelers coming for him. They definitely possessed magic, and understanding their plans would help considerably when they arrived tomorrow.

He needed to speak with Artino now, though, so he headed downstairs to the laboratory.

He didn't knock but walked right through the door.

"Always! Always interrupting me!" Artino shouted, throwing his hands into the air and the papers he was holding as well. "Ridiculous, Rendal! You need to announce yourself! Create appointments! I have *work* to do!"

"I know, I know." Rendal walked into the room, stopping a few feet from Artino's desk. "It's okay, Artino. I don't plan on being here long. I need to talk to you about what you showed me."

"Yes. I showed it to you. What else is there to talk about?"

Artino started pacing again, staring at the floor and refusing to look Rendal in the eye.

"How quickly can we operationalize it?"

Artino stopped but didn't look up. "What do you mean, Rendal? What are you saying?"

"How quickly can I have an army?"

Artino's feet started moving quickly, pacing in a figure eight. "He wants an army now. I just gave him genius, and he wants an army. It's unending. I shouldn't have ever taken this assignment. He's mad, I tell you. Mad! *Mad.*"

Rendal didn't care what the man was saying; he only needed an answer. "*Artino,* it's a simple question. How long before we can operationalize the technology?"

"I don't know, Rendal. You've drained all the subjects of their nanocytes. The man over there, he's the only one with a full measure. The nanocytes will have to replicate, and that takes time. You know that. I can't just put bracelets on people, and expect this start working. It's going to take time."

"How *much* time? That's what I need to know."

"A month."

Rendal's hand turned into a fist. "No, Artino. It must be shorter than that. If I need them tomorrow, how many can you give me?"

Artino laughed, a high, strained thing that made it sound like something inside the man was near to breaking. "None. I can give you none except that man over here."

Rendal looked into the corner. The man hadn't appeared to move since Rendal saw him earlier. "Is he even alive?"

"Yes, yes. I take the bracelet off of him routinely, with a guard. Feed him, allow him to use the bathroom. He's fine. He's all you will get, Rendal, at least for now. If you want more, you're going to have to stop *draining* them upstairs. You understand?"

Rendal ignored the little man. One would not be enough, at least not to do real damage. They were bringing a few handfuls of people. Rendal could handle them easily, magic or no. He would have to decide whether he wanted to use this man, but he was leaning toward not doing so. Perhaps keep him in the pocket for now. After all, this was only the first skirmish.

"Okay, Artino. Don't have an aneurysm. We will use him, and I will slow down the draining. Just make more bracelets. Do you understand?"

"Yes, yes. I understand. I always understand. If you'd only quit interrupting me!"

Rendal was smiling as he left the room. He thoroughly enjoyed disrupting Artino's day. It always made him feel great.

CHAPTER NINETEEN

"You tired?" Worth asked.

William shook his head. A lie, but a necessary one. The truth was, he was exhausted. Tomorrow they'd finish their journey, and William's life the past two weeks had been nothing if not overworked. The past three nights he'd slept maybe six hours total, and now he was a few hours away from dawn without much hope of any sleep.

Still, this had to be done.

"It okay be tired." Worth patted him on the back. "Now, tomorrow. It okay. Battle come. No tired. Bloodlust then. You be fine."

The tent city leader talked as if he were William's superior, and in the beginning, William had despised it.

Now, on the last night, he thought Worth might be. He would *never* tell that to anyone, of course, but the man had wisdom that his horrible grammar and goofy nature didn't reveal.

And he was right. William *was* tired, and he would be

tired tomorrow—but when the war came, his body and mind would react. They always did.

"He watch us." Worth nodded. "Yes. Now. He watching us."

"Rendal?"

Worth looked to him. "That his name? Mage?"

"Yes."

Worth looked to his left and right. "Yes. He see us. Good. Let him. We come for him. We get woman back."

He looked at William.

"We almost done. You sleep next, aye?"

"Almost done?"

"Aye. Almost done. With this. There more, but this almost done."

William didn't believe him, but what could he say? He was at the tent city leader's direction.

"Then stop slowing us down with chit-chat, Worth. Get to the point."

Worth smiled and stepped back. "Bossy boss, aye. Okay. Go on."

William's eyes widened. "Go on? Go on where?"

"Make fire. Make magic. On sword. We almost done."

William laughed, then looked at the sleeping campsite to see if anyone heard him. No one stirred. He turned back to Worth. "We've been able to make my hands light up a bit. We're nowhere near me doing what you did with the sword."

"You—" Worth pointed to his own head. "Wood for brains. You. Go on. Make fire. Make magic. On sword."

William wanted to throw the damn thing at him. He held it in his hands, the point touching the ground. Last night, he'd managed to get to a place where he could bring flames to his hands about half the times he tried. He was starting to understand the focus—where to place it, and how to feed it.

That was a far, far cry from what Worth was saying now.

"I back up. You might burn me." Worth smiled as he said it, and William saw glee in his eyes. He was serious about this; he wasn't fucking around.

The man went back about thirty feet, leaving open space between them.

William was basically alone and didn't know what the hell to do.

"Fuck you, Worth," he grumbled.

William supposed they could stand here until Worth grew tired and came back, because that was about all that would happen.

The tent city leader didn't move, and William remained alone, holding his sword.

And not trying.

He let out a deep sigh. This wasn't about him or his ego. It was about Riley, and Worth was right, even if he wasn't saying it: they were out of time. If William was to augment his fighting with magic, he had to get it together tonight.

Because tomorrow, war came.

He closed his eyes and remembered the things Worth had taught him in his broken language.

Only broken you, he remembered Worth telling him. *Me understand fine. Me speak good.*

William smiled, forgetting himself for a moment.

When Riley sees this, he thought, *she's gonna piss her pants.*

She can talk all the shit she wants about being a better swords-man, but she won't have fire attached to her blade, will she?

He forgot himself a bit more.

And Rendal? That evil fucking wannabe mage? When he understands that it doesn't matter how many men he sends my way, they'll just be decapitated by a sword of flames? I can't wait to see his face. I can't wait.

And just a bit more of William's ego left.

Faces started flashing through William's mind. Those he cared about. Those he would kill tomorrow. Goland. Mason. Worth. Torney. Rendal. Harold.

Riley.

William felt the fire on his hands, but he'd felt that before.

It was Worth's hoot from across the expanse that made him open his eyes.

He looked at the tent city leader first. Worth was dancing in the darkness, trotting around like a child. William tipped his head down and saw his hands—on fire as he thought they would be—but that wasn't all...

His sword was ablaze.

Fire wrapped around it, up and down, covering the hilt and blade.

William's eyes grew wide.

"Hit me, wood for brains!" Worth shouted.

William's head jerked up, and he thought the fire would go out. He looked back at it, but it still burned.

"It part of you, wood for brains! You magic. It same as sword. Part of *you!*"

He was shouting loudly now, not caring about waking up those still sleeping. William turned to the campsite again; no one was lying down. They were all standing and staring at him. At his sword.

Mason walked to the front.

"I bet Riley could do that, no problem!" Mason shouted to him.

William laughed, actually feeling good. "Go fuck yourself, Assistant Prefect!"

He lifted the sword, a giant, heavy thing to most people, but the only tool he went to work with each morning. He could feel the fire's heat on his face, although it didn't burn his hands.

I'll give them a show, William thought. *If that's what they want.*

He swung his sword with both hands as if he were about to slice deep through someone's ribcage. It was a move he'd executed countless times before, but he felt something different this time. His sword was no longer limited to the metal it'd been created from.

It was extended by the fire that wreathed it.

He swung it *farther.*

The fire swept through the air rapidly and Worth dropped to the ground, the flames barely missing him. William stared at him, hardly able to believe what he was seeing. Worth was still hooting from the ground, yelling from either pain or happiness—it was hard to tell.

"You magic!"

"I'm magic!" William roared into the night air.

"You're a popular person, Right Hand."

Rendal stood in front of Riley's doorway.

She looked up to him. "What are you talking about?"

"They're coming for you."

"Who?" She didn't stand from the bed but it looked like she was about to, always reaching for that nonexistent sword.

"New Perth. There are quite a few of them this time. The other Right Hand, plus some people I don't recognize. Mutants, from the looks of them. From the Badlands. One other man who appears to be from New Perth. And then, of course, Mason. Your precious Assistant Prefect."

She *did* stand up then, and Rendal understood fully how much she cared for that man. She would do *anything* for him if she thought it was in his best interest.

Rendal wanted to smile but didn't. He saw the path through this now, even if he hadn't in the very beginning. The goal was in front of him: Riley Trident. The path? Well, that would be revealed to everyone very soon.

"Yes, he's coming. They should be here this evening."

"What are you going to do?"

"I'm going to politely ask them to leave, of course," Rendal replied. "Then everything will be fine, yes?"

Her eyes narrowed. He could venture into her mind and know what she was thinking, but he thought that might be a bit dangerous. Rendal was coming to understand how powerful this woman was the longer that he remained around her. Even after only a few days, he thought she was coming to know when he was reading her thoughts.

"Don't hurt them. I'll do what you want. I'll stay here. Just don't hurt them."

"I'm going to bring Lucie out for the meeting with them." He said nothing else for a second, letting that sink in. "You haven't seen the truth of my words yet, but you will soon. Perhaps after tomorrow. However, I know how dangerous you are with your hands—even without that sword. Lucie will be there in case for some reason you decide to...forget what side you're on now. Do you understand, Riley?"

The woman swallowed. She was quiet for a long second, then, "I understand."

"Good. Now, when they arrive there will be a bit of talking, I imagine. But not too much. They're disrespecting the deal we made: that if you came with me, I would leave them in peace. They're bringing war to me, and I have to protect my people. I'm sure you understand. What I want from you is to tell them to leave, that you're fine here. That you want to be here."

"They know that's not true, Rendal."

"Fine. They can know whatever they want," Rendal said. "It's your job to convince them. You say that you want to be here, and maybe they'll leave unhurt. If you don't convince them with your words, then I will with my own type of persuasion."

Rendal couldn't help himself then, venturing slightly into her mind.

He only remained there for a second. It was all hate and anger, nothing else, and all of it directed at him.

"If you hurt them, I'm going to kill you." Riley's voice was cold steel. "I don't care what it takes. What I have to do. I will murder you. I need you to understand that deep in your bones. If you hurt those I care about, you will be hurt next."

"Everyone talks, Riley. Everyone always talks. You know what I like best about Harold? He understands that talk doesn't matter. Action does. Today, if your friends won't listen to reason, you'll see my action. You can talk, but after this evening, I think you'll have a lot less to say."

Harold came to Riley's door next, hours later.

"He's ready for you."

"And he sends *you*?" Riley stood up.

"I do as he wishes, yes."

"For how long?"

Harold smiled. "Until someone more powerful comes, of course."

"He knows that?"

"I imagine he knows everything, but we are spending too much time talking. Come. Your friends are almost here."

Riley felt helpless, and she hated that. She had *never* felt helpless but had always possessed the power to do something. Now she didn't.

"Here." Harold stepped forward holding one of those green necklaces in his hands. "You're to wear this, so we don't have any more mishaps like before."

He reached out to put it on her.

"No." Her voice was icy steel. "I'll put it on. You can check it after. Don't put your hands near me."

She'd been left without restraints or one of these necklaces since just after he'd first captured her, Rendal clearly feeling he could handle her if he wanted to. She sure as hell wasn't letting this cretin touch her.

Harold studied her face for a second, obviously deciding whether he wanted the hassle of a fight.

He handed the necklace over. He didn't.

Smart of him, she thought.

Riley took the necklace and put it on, latching the back together. Harold moved behind her.

"Good. Now, upstairs we go. You first, Right Hand."

Riley walked, unsure what to expect. She knew what was expected of *her*. That had been made explicitly clear earlier in the day. Give the party line. Do not try to attack. Watch as her friends are decimated—and that *is* what would happen. She held no doubt about that.

She could preach for hours about how much she loved Rendal and his compound. How it was a fucking dream.

William wouldn't believe it.

Mason wouldn't believe it.

And they would attack. Regardless of who else was with them, those two wouldn't hold back.

Then what would she do? She didn't give a damn about the necklace. The magic that had erupted from her before had acted on its own accord. What she needed were her hands, and these fools apparently weren't going to chain her.

That was a serious mistake on their part, although she understood why they were making it: she couldn't very well sing Rendal's praises while in chains.

But if her hands were free to move, people were free to die.

Lucie, she thought.

The man was evil, no doubt about that, but he was also highly intelligent. Cunning. He'd thought through so many possible outcomes, and he knew all the angles.

Instinct, then—that was what Riley would have to rely on. She would have to see the lay of the battlefield, how the separate armies were positioned, and then make her decision to attack or to stay silent. To hold her friends' lives or Lucie's in higher regard.

They reached the compound's large front doors. Rendal was in front, waiting for them to open.

"Have you heard your friends calling?" He didn't turn around.

It was only the three of them—Rendal, Riley, and Harold.

"No," Riley answered.

"Remember, if you do as I say, Lucie lives. If you try to fight she will die, along with your friends. There will be no winner here except me."

Riley was silent. Rendal flipped his hand, and the doors in front of him started moving. He wore two bracelets now, although she didn't understand why. One was green, the color she'd seen over and over since showing up here. The other was a deep red.

As the door opened, light poured in from outside—the rays of a falling sun. It was nearly dusk.

The green bracelet lit up, the red one remaining a dull red.

What is it? she wondered. *What's it do for him?*

"Harold, please take your position."

"Yes, sir."

Harold walked behind Riley, leaving the incoming light. Riley shielded her eyes for a moment as the door opened fully.

Rendal went first and Riley followed, her eyes adjusting. She looked to her left and right at soldiers in a huge semi-circle. She thought there must have been a hundred on either side. Riley quickly looked at the top of the compound behind her, finding the archers she was looking for.

Her mind had flipped into war mode without any direction from her, understanding the layout and where all parties were situated. Her training was taking over, and there was nothing she—or *Rendal*—could do about it.

Before her stood fourteen people. Their shadows lay across the dirt as the sun dropped beneath the horizon. Mason was in the middle… *Stupid, stupid, stupid*, Riley thought. She wanted him behind the line and to the left since she thought that would be the hardest place for the archers to see.

She understood why he wasn't, though.

He was the Assistant Prefect, head representative from New Perth, and to hide in the back was beneath that position, and him.

William stood to his right, and Verith to his left. Spread out on either side were people she didn't know. Rendal had been right; they were mutants. People with growths in places that shouldn't have any, and bare spaces where they should have body parts. Riley had heard of people like them, descendants of the long-ago wars. She'd never seen one before and had no idea why they would be here now.

"Rendal Hemmons, as Assistant Prefect from New

Perth, I command you to release our Right Hand. If you do so, we will return without violence. If you refuse, the power of New Perth will fall upon you."

Rendal stopped, and Riley did too. They were alone, the soldiers fifty feet away and Mason another thirty in front of them.

Rendal turned around, looking at the archers perched above him.

"It seems that the power is on my side, Assistant Prefect. Not to mention, you're breaking our deal. You give your Right Hand to me, and I leave New Perth alone. Now you bring war to my place?"

"Release her," William called, "or I'm going to bury my sword so far up your ass you'll think you ate steel for dinner!"

"Everyone talks," Rendal said quietly. He turned slightly to Riley. "Your turn."

Riley didn't know where Lucie was. She hadn't seen her so far, but that didn't mean the woman wasn't here.

Riley stepped forward, her hands at her sides. Her senses were insanely perceptive, feeling everything around her. Her hands kept wanting to reach for the sword that no longer resided on her hip.

It doesn't matter what I say here, she thought.

"Mason," she called loud enough to cross the distance between them. "William. You both need to leave. I've made my choice, and it's here. With him. There's nothing you can do about it, so please—" She felt real emotion then, needing them to understand she wanted them to leave. "*Please*, go. There's nothing for you here. I'm not leaving."

"He didn't put any chains on you, Riley, but I can see

that green necklace the same as I can see you." William's voice was louder than hers. "He doesn't want that magic bursting out, does he? Wants to keep you nice and safe. I gotta say, Rendal, someone wearing that magic necklace doesn't seem like they really want to be there to me. Seems like you're fuckin' keeping her there against her will."

Rendal turned his back on them, glancing at her as he did. "You did well. Now they make their own choice."

Riley watched him start walking back toward the door, his robe billowing slightly as he did.

"Fuck it," she whispered.

If her friends were going to die today, she would too.

She rushed forward, her feet deadly messengers, their message the person they carried. She made almost no sound as she reached the mage, jumping into the air, her hands outstretched to take him down in a devastating roll.

Rendal turned just before she hit him, his eyes red and his hands in a cupped position, pointing at her.

Fire blazed out, a flood of it.

Riley knew at that moment that she was dead.

Yet she watched as the fire spread out around her as if hitting some field she couldn't see.

"Silly mage!"

The voice came from behind her, and Riley realized she wasn't falling but hanging in midair.

The soldiers behind Rendal rushed forward, their horses' hooves like thunder.

Riley was being pulled backward, moving through the air inside some invisible field. Rendal was no longer throwing fire at her; he'd turned to the man who had shouted. The people around Mason were spreading out now, and—

"*NO FUCKING WAY!*" Riley shouted with an amazed smile.

Fire engulfed William's sword.

Riley was still moving backward, although she didn't know who was controlling her.

The archers had let their first round of arrows fly and were now reloading.

Riley knew everyone was dead, just as she'd known she was dead moments before. They had no shields, no protection at all from the metal speeding to pierce them.

Riley's eye caught a woman on the far right. She was moving her hands in an odd way at the arrows streaking through the air.

The arrows coalesced as they got closer to their targets—and then they simply *burst*. Not apart, but their metal tips went every which way, some simply fluttering to the ground while others were flung far into the distance. They were no longer a threat.

"Wind," Riley whispered. "She used concentrated wind to scatter them."

Riley touched the ground, and whatever was holding her dissipated. She was twenty feet behind Mason, who was marching forward with his own sword drawn.

"*MASON! NO!*"

He turned around and looked at her. Her senses were still focused, but now only on him. He wasn't supposed to be out here. He was a Prefect, meant to command troops, not be one.

Her feet flew, rushing across the ground towards her commander.

"Go. Get out of here. I'll stay and fight."

He laughed. Actually laughed at her as screams rang out across the expanse.

"I didn't come here to run back home, Riley. You want my sword or this hand-axe? We're going to kill this fucker."

She looked beyond him. So many things were happening that she couldn't focus on any single event—and right now she had to figure out how to protect Mason.

"What weapon are you best at?" she asked.

"Probably the sword."

"Give me the axe then, and listen to me, you damn fool. Stay behind me at all times. Fucking *behind* me, you got that?"

He smiled, looking like a mischievous boy. "Yeah, I got you."

She grabbed the axe, immediately feeling safer. She hadn't known how much she'd missed having a weapon in her hand. How much like *home* it felt.

She surveyed the scene. William was on the left, and she so did not want to hear him bragging when this was finished. His flame-enshrouded sword was flinging fire across the land, killing multiple adversaries at once. There were people with him, although none were using weapons. Riley could hardly understand what she was looking at, but it appeared to be a mixture of flames, rocks, and…

"That's not possible," she whispered.

A flock of birds was descending on the group to the left, but only on Rendal's men. They were screeching, pecking, and clawing, raking the flesh from Mason's enemies.

On the right of Rendal was another group. Verith was with them, and although he didn't have fire attached to his sword, he still wielded his steel brilliantly. Riley saw flames everywhere, dirt and rocks flying from the ground, and what looked to be electricity ripping through the air.

And in the middle? Rendal stood, his eyes red and his hands wide to his side.

The bald man who had screamed earlier was approaching him, his hands at his hips, palms facing the mage.

"You magic, aye? Me magic too."

Rendal brought his left hand up and sent out a bolt of fire, and the big bald man dodged it easily, simply moving his shoulder as if someone had swung at him.

"That magic? Ha!"

He kept moving forward.

Rendal's right hand attacked next, shooting out tiny flakes of fire, arrowheads that streaked over the ground.

The bald man raised his left hand and electricity sparked from it—bright and shining like static in the night. He shot it forward, long strands lacing over one another and forming a net. The fire plunged into it.

"Silly mage!"

The bald man was nearly to Rendal now.

Riley saw the green wristband get brighter.

"No," she whispered. "We've got to help him."

Rendal brought both hands together, and a thunderous roar rolled across the expanse.

The bald man brought his other hand up, but whatever he'd wanted to do with it didn't matter. He flew back as if struck by a titan-sized fist. He hit the ground hard, skidding across the dirt. He scrambled to gain traction, his left hand still sparking with electricity.

Rendal turned, the bracelet on his wrist still burning bright. The sun was descending further, and the green looked even more menacing. Rendal watched his hundred soldiers being decimated by five people.

"No." He waved his hand.

The five were scattered as if a giant had reached down and overturned a game board.

"Fuck this." Riley had had enough. "Stay here, Mason."

Rendal started turning to the other side and Riley lunged forward, knowing she'd already waited too long. The axe was in her right hand, and her arms pumped wildly. In the coming darkness, she looked almost like a ghost—not truly there, ethereal in her speed. Her peripheral vision showed her that William was still wreaking havoc and that he didn't see what was coming for him.

Rendal's left hand started sweeping up from the side, ready to decimate the small group.

Riley's right arm moved like a slingshot, barely able to be seen. The axe flew from her fingers, flipping end over end.

It hit home just as Rendal was starting to flick his wrist.

It split his shoulder, digging deep and pushing him over. He slid to the ground, whatever spell he'd been casting broken.

"FUCK!" he shouted, looking at his wound.

Riley didn't stop running toward him. She was only twenty feet away now and closing.

Rendal didn't climb to his feet, but simply *levitated*, his body lifting off the ground until he was upright.

Stop.

The voice filled her head—*his* voice.

Or Lucie dies.

Riley planted her feet, skidding across the dirt. With his uninjured arm, the mage pointed behind him, behind the archers atop the compound. Lucie floated above them, the green necklace visible in the fading light.

The red bracelet caught Riley's eye as it lit up on Rendal's wrist.

Suddenly fire roared out from her left, so hot it nearly blistered her skin. Riley fell to the ground, shielding her face but still able to see what was happening.

Someone else was there, clearly—someone she had never seen before. He looked brain-dead, his eyes staring into the carnage blankly, his face lax. A red necklace rested on his neck while fire blazed from his hands, and *everyone* had been scattered, both Rendal's men and those Mason had brought. Fire roared across the ground, burning on dry weeds and dead twigs. It burned on people, good and bad alike. The man kept pouring it from his hands.

"You see, Riley?" Rendal stepped forward, pulling the axe out of his arm. He grimaced and dropped it to the ground. "There's no way to stop me. Not you or your little friends. New Perth is mine. It's *always* been mine. None of you realized it until now."

Riley saw his eyes flick behind her.

Mason!

"Yes, Mason. The one you care for above all else."

Riley rose to her feet nearly as quickly as the mage had.

"You'll have to go through me."

Riley felt the heat growing closer on her left, and the sounds of the struggle died away.

"Riley!" William shouted. "Run!"

She didn't turn to the sound of his voice but kept her eyes on the mage.

"Join me, Riley. Join me now, and all of this can end. Because this bracelet on my wrist, the red one? That's the fire you feel, even if you don't understand it. Join me, and I'll let you all live. If you don't, everyone here will die right now."

Riley understood that he was telling the truth, and she also understood she'd made a mistake by agreeing to come here, to begin with. There would be no peace with this man. He wanted New Perth, and he meant to have it no matter what.

Riley looked down at her feet; the fire was still growing hotter and spreading farther and farther. She could hear William's grunts, fighting soldiers even as the flames grew closer to him. She could sense people standing on her right, bones broken from how the mage had sent them sprawling.

The bald man with magic was slowly standing behind her.

Her body and mind focused on trying to find a way out of this. A way she could stop this evil man and save her friends.

The hand-axe lay discarded on the ground in front of her.

Okay, Riley. One chance. Make it count.

She launched herself, a blur in the darkness. She saw the mage's hand moving, trying to keep up with her long enough to shoot something deadly her way. Riley slid across the ground, grabbing the axe with her right hand and stopping her slide with her left. She swung, a shot aiming directly at the back of the man's knee.

An inch from connecting, she was propelled into the air and watched with growing horror as Mason was pulled toward Rendal.

"Nice try," the mage quipped as he wrapped his arm around Mason's throat, a small blade in his hand.

Riley remained frozen in the air.

"This isn't over, Right Hand. In fact, it's just getting started."

"*MASON!*" Riley shouted from twenty feet in the air.

A blinding light flashed from where Rendal stood, spreading out and masking everything else around it. One second, the bright light was there, and the next it was gone.

The mage was no more. Mason was no more. They were both gone.

Riley fell, landing without injury. Dust floated up around her. She wasted no time, lunging to where Mason had been.

The fire on the left had stopped growing, but she cared nothing for that. She looked wildly around her, trying to find Mason; trying to understand where he could have gone.

The soldiers were fleeing, running since their leader was now gone.

Riley saw all of this, but not where *her* leader was. She couldn't see Mason anywhere.

William jogged up, his huge feet shaking the ground. "Where are they? Where did he go?"

The bald man—Riley still didn't know his name—moved closer. "He gone. Teleport."

"What the fuck are you talking about?" Riley shrieked. "WHERE DID HE GO?"

"There," the bald man pointed. Riley turned around, dust, smoke, and flames partly clouding her vision. A large boat was pulling out from behind the compound. "That him. He there."

Riley's eyes flashed to the top of the compound. Lucie was there, discarded just as the axe had been.

And then she understood. He'd planned this. The mage had lured them all here, every single one of them, and for what?

To get Mason.

And now he had him. The compound was deserted—she felt sure of that, at least every part of the compound that mattered. Rendal was gone, Harold with him.

And Mason.

Riley fell to her knees, tears flooding her eyes.

William was at her side. "It's okay, Riley. Listen to me. It's okay. We're going to get him back, just like we got you back."

She shook her head, hardly hearing the big man. "He's one step ahead. He's always one step ahead."

CHAPTER TWENTY

The boat rocked slightly with the waves. It was a large boat so Harold couldn't feel the rocking motion much, but he hated what he did feel. He'd been on the boat for two nights, and he woke up each night with the slightest tossing.

He'd been called to his master now, and Harold thought it couldn't possibly be a good thing.

Rendal's room on the boat was the largest, nearly the size of three regular rooms.

"Harold, welcome. Please, have a seat."

Rendal was lounging on a large couch, blowing smoke rings. He held no cigarette or tobacco pipe, he was simply blowing them.

In the back corner, Harold saw Mason Ire. The Assistant Prefect. He was chained, and glared at Harold. He wore no green necklace, meaning Rendal saw no magical threat from him.

Harold made his way to the chair that was clearly for

him. It sat in the middle of the room with nothing around it.

He sat down.

"Harold, you've been loyal to me for a long time, and I've appreciated that loyalty. Truly. You've helped me build this enterprise as much as anyone else. I don't want you to think I don't recognize that, you know?"

"Yes, sir." Harold didn't move an inch.

"I know that you've been wondering things lately, Harold. You follow power, and that's one of the reasons I've felt so secure in our relationship. I know me, and I know my capabilities. New Perth is just the beginning. I know there is no one more powerful, but you've had doubts lately, haven't you?"

This room was no longer safe, and Harold knew it.

"The woman is powerful."

"Indeed, she is." Rendal blew a giant smoke ring, watching it spread through the air. "That's why I want her, Harold. But you've been doubting me; doubting whether I was more powerful."

"It is true. It is my nature. I cannot help it."

"I know, buddy. That's why I don't blame you. That's why I called you here instead of throwing you over the side. We can't help who we are. But you and I, we need to talk. To come to an understanding, okay?"

"Yes, sir." Harold watched a smoke ring hit the ceiling and spread to nothing.

"I need you to consider what just happened. To truly consider it."

Rendal sat up.

"The girl burnt me before, did she not?"

"She did."

"And do you see burns on my skin now?"

"No, sir." And Harold didn't. The mage had healed perfectly.

"And behind me, do you see New Perth's royalty chained up?"

"I do."

"And why is he chained? Why do I have him and not the woman? Do you think she escaped again?"

"I...I don't know, sir."

Rendal nodded and stood. "I know you don't, and that's what we need to talk about. You have begun doubting my power, yet you don't understand what's happening around you. Let me ask, Harold—did you realize that I had been building the necessary technology into this ship? The same technology that was in the compound?"

"No, sir."

"No, you didn't. You had no idea because I did it without your knowledge. I used *other* people for it and kept you in the dark. And now we're on this ship, and true, I couldn't bring everyone, but I have enough soldiers and prisoners to continue basically as if nothing happened. Even better, New Perth won't know where I am."

Harold nodded, absolutely certain he wasn't seeing everything yet.

"I'll introduce you soon to the person in charge of that feat. I won't hide her from you. But my point is, you don't see everything that I do. Your vantage point isn't wide enough. You see only the piece I allow you."

Rendal turned and looked at the Assistant Prefect.

"Case in point: do you know why he's here?"

Harold shook his head.

"Guess."

"You want to use him for ransom."

Rendal sighed. "No, Harold. No, not at all. You see? You questioning my power is like an ant questioning a god's power. You see nothing. I have this man here because *he* is the way to Riley's heart. *He* is how I will bend her to my will. She's powerful, goodness, yes. But like you, she can't see as far as I can. All that nonsense outside the compound last evening? That was show, my friend. I only wanted him. I didn't care about keeping Riley or I would have locked her up in the ship. I wanted *her* to see me take him."

He turned back to Harold.

"I want her to understand there's no hope. That her *only* chance of peace is joining me. Do you see that?"

Harold nodded. He did.

"We are not at the end but the beginning, and the game will be a long one. From this boat, we'll move to the next stage, and in the end, the Right Hand will stand by my side and do my bidding. The question I need you to answer, Harold, is where you're going to be in all this? Are you with me, or do you think she's more powerful?"

Harold glanced at the silent Mason and back at Rendal.

Harold had been wrong. The woman could not beat this man, this mage. Everything bent to his will, even if it took some longer than others. Eventually, they would fall.

"Forgive me, master." Harold dropped to his knees. "I serve you."

"Good, Harold. Good. I'm glad to keep you around. You're a valuable member of this team, and I'd hate to see you leave. Now, stand. I want you and Mason here to come see my new army. One of the reasons I was able to leave so many people behind."

Rendal smiled wildly as he reached down and took Harold's hand, lifting him up.

Riley held the sword in her hand. She stared at it intently, with a focus that predators in the wild would understand.

She placed one finger under the base of the blade, right where it met the hilt.

It balanced perfectly, not swaying at all.

Three men stood behind her, all of them silent. Riley wasn't paying them any attention, but truthfully, two of them were somewhat frightened.

William and Goland.

The woman who stood in front of them wasn't the woman they'd known a month ago, and the intensity in the room now was beyond uncomfortable.

"When you magic," Worth told her, "sword be magic too. You magic…or you will be. You be magic soon."

Riley nodded, her back still to them.

Her previous sword—her fucking *lifeline*—was gone, and Worth had spent the past three days creating this. He'd gone to New Perth's blacksmith, and according to the blacksmith, hadn't stopped working for seventy-two solid hours. Now this sword was in her hand.

"It's magic, huh, Worth?"

"Aye. When *you* magic, it magic."

The blacksmith said Worth had done, "All manner of crazy shit 'round that melted steel. I don't know nothin' 'bout what he was doin', so don't blame me if that thing breaks."

And now Riley held his work in her hands. It didn't feel like her last sword, but then, no two swords were ever the same.

Something was different about it, though. She could tell that much. Green lines ran through the sword's hilt.

Riley knew what they looked like: Rendal's bracelets and necklaces.

She didn't give a single fuck, because she trusted Worth. She had seen him throw electricity at Rendal and witnessed his loved ones die. If he said this sword was fucking magic, then it was fucking magic.

She turned around, sheathing the sword at her side, and stepped forward.

"The horses are still in the stables, right? Wind Whisper and Broadsword?" She knew they were here; she'd helped bring them back, but part of her wanted to make sure again. That Rendal hadn't stolen them *and* Mason.

"We got 'em,' Riley," William told her. "They're safe."

She looked at the Prefect and fell to one knee.

"I have failed you, Your Grace. I did not protect your son, and I therefore offer you my resignation as Right Hand. I do not deserve to serve you or your family."

"Oh, Riley, get up. Get up right now. You're not resigning anything." Goland pulled on her purple robe, raising her to her feet.

She met his eyes. "Are you sure?"

"Of course, I'm sure, Riley."

She sighed and looked at her feet. "That's good, because if you *had* accepted I was going to steal one of New Perth's boats and go get him anyway. I just figured I didn't want to break laws if I didn't have to."

William snorted. "And then *I'd* have to break laws, because I'm goin' with you, skinny. You might have a magic sword, but I'm the one with fire. You're going to need it."

She looked at him. "We're getting him back. Do you understand that? We're getting Mason back, and we're going to kill Rendal."

"Oh, I understand. The only thing I'm concerned about is you admitting it in the end when my body count is higher than yours. I need someone to count fair, and I don't trust Worth over here."

"Worth count good, wood-for-brains."

"I'll beat you, chubby. I have no doubt about that, but there's one other thing you need to understand. Two names. Belarus and Rendal. *I* kill them both."

"Fine by me, skinny, but enough jibber-jabber. We need to get movin'."

Riley turned to Worth. "Thank you for this weapon."

"Thank later. Now we go."

"We?" Riley's eyebrows raised.

"Yes. We. More tent people come. More magic. We move to New Perth. We help, aye?"

Riley looked at Goland. "What's he talking about?"

"I worked it out with him." The Prefect nodded. "He and his clan are moving to New Perth. We have another eighty mages coming to help us. Thirty are already here."

Riley closed her eyes, smiling broadly. "Rendal doesn't stand a fucking chance."

FINIS

First, I'd like to say thanks for trying out this new series! It means the world to me (and Michael) that you were willing to venture into a new land with us.

It was really exciting writing this book, and a major reason for that was leaving the area that most of the Age of Magic takes place in. With this series, we were exploring how other parts of Earth had evolved and changed since the WWDE.

The other reason I enjoyed this book so much was learning about Riley. I think she's different than some of the other female leads inside the Age of Magic. She's still a badass, but she doesn't *fully* believe in that badass-ness yet. I also fell in love with her sense of duty, her willingness to sacrifice everything for both Mason and New Perth.

I'm looking forward to going deeper with Riley and her crew; I think Rendal is a worthy opponent, if completely fucking evil. He's crafty as well as powerful, and I think he's got a lot more tricks up his sleeve.

I've done my best here to mimic Michael's style while

also keeping the story fresh and interesting. Too often when you have co-authors (not in Michael's world, he takes great care with his books), stories can get redundant, with the exact same thing happening in each book. What I wanted to do here was bring the excitement, humor, and sense of adventure that permeates Michael's own writing, but throw some new ideas into it.

I'm really excited about where this story is going. I think the Right Hands are going to have their hand's full (UH-MAZING PUN!) with Rendal, and Riley's definitely going to need to be able to use her magic if they're going to have a chance. Will she be able to unleash the power inside her?

If you enjoyed this book, PLEASE leave a review. Michael and I are independent authors, and each 5-star review really does help us move units!

Thanks again, and I can't wait to continue you this journey with the Right Hands as well as you!

All the best,
Jace

AUTHOR NOTES - MICHAEL ANDERLE

DECEMBER 4, 2018

THANK YOU for not only reading this story but these *Author Notes* as well.

(I think I've been good with always opening with "thank you." If not, I need to edit the other *Author Notes*!)

RANDOM (*sometimes*) THOUGHTS?

From Jace's *Author Notes*: "I think Rendal is a worthy opponent, if completely fucking evil."

I laughed out loud (in a restaurant) when I read that line. But then I wondered, what is "completely fucking evil?"

Is evil (like porn) something that "you know it when you see it?" Is it the act of killing sentient beings the ultimate in evil? Well, we would argue no (think wars) when you know the other side has decent people, but they are throwing lead at you, so you throw lead back at them.

We *know* that isn't completely fucking evil.

Does it (in the end) boil down to the capability of someone to ignore all repercussions (including death and destruction) on their way to their goals? If so, then is it just the act of ignoring all repercussions enough to say someone is completely fucking evil?

For example, if someone is so truly focused on their goal that they have no second thoughts about possible repercussions evil?

Or was it that sometimes normal, non-evil persons act like someone who is completely fucking evil and only by good luck, fortune, or grace nothing horrible happens and their moment of evilness is never unveiled?

Damn, I need to drink more Coke and not ponder this deep stuff so often. I'll bet you it's the tea I'm drinking.

HOW TO MARKET FOR BOOKS YOU LOVE

We are able to support our efforts with you reading our books, and we appreciate you doing this!

If you enjoyed this or ANY book by any author, especially Indie-published, we always appreciate if you make the time to review a book, since it lets other readers who might be on the fence to take a chance on it as well.

AROUND THE WORLD IN 80 DAYS

One of the interesting (at least to me) aspects of my life is my ability to work from anywhere and at any time. In the future, I hope to re-read my own *Author Notes* and remember my life as a diary entry.

Dinner at Five50 (Aria Hotel Pizza Place)

So, I left the Vegas Condo office to finish work down here in Five50. For whatever reason, I can often work here for hours and the time just melts away in the background.

The service is good, and the tea (I think) has a boost of caffeine a lot of tea doesn't contain. Some nights, I'll sit here and work for a few hours and then be up all night until 2:00 in the morning.

I have Five50 tea to blame.

On or around the 23rd of December, I'll be traveling to La Puente (LA area) for Christmas, and then getting on a plane to Australia (and a 20Books event in Adelaide!) for New Year's. Then on to Bali for a 20Books event on January 4th.

I'm hoping the trips will provide more fodder for my active imagination and I'll be able to bring new and fresh content to you for years to come.

FAN PRICING

If you would like to find out what LMBPN is doing and the books we will be publishing, just sign up at http:// lmbpn.com/email/. When you sign up, we notify you of books coming out for the week, any new posts of interest in the books and pop culture arena, and the fan pricing on Saturday.

Ad Aeternitatem,

Michael Anderle

THE RISE OF MAGIC

with CM Raymond and LE Barbant

Restriction (1) – Reawakening (2) – Rebellion (3) – Revolution (4) – Unlawful Passage (5) – Darkness Rises (6) – The Gods Beneath (7) – Reborn (8)

STORMS OF MAGIC

with PT Hylton

Storm Raiders (1) – Storm Callers (2) – Storm Breakers (3) – Storm Warrior (4)

TALES OF THE FEISTY DRUID

with Candy Crum

The Arcadian Druid (1) – The Undying Illusionist (2) – The Frozen Wasteland (3) – The Deceiver (4) – The Lost (5) – The Damned (6) – Into The Maelstrom (7)

A NEW DAWN

with Amy Hopkins

Dawn of Destiny (1) – Dawn of Darkness (2) – Dawn of Deliverance (3) – Dawn of Days (4) – Broken Skies (5) – Broken Bones (6)

TALES OF THE WELLSPRING KNIGHT

with P.J. Cherubino

Knight's Creed (1) – Knight's Struggle (2) – Knight's Justice (3) - Etheric Knight (4)

THE HIDDEN MAGIC CHRONICLES

with Justin Sloan

Shades of Light (1) – Shades of Dark (2) – Shades of Glory (3) – Shades of Justice (4)

PATH OF HEROES

with Brandon Barr

Rogue Mage (1)